"You're out of a job. You realize that don't you?"

He didn't give her time to answer his rhetorical question. "And I won't be conveniently supporting my niece from a convenient distance. Close up and personal. That's the role I intend to play." His mouth was a grim line.

"I can survive happily without your money," Vicky bit out sharply. "I've managed on my own for years and I can carry on managing." She could feel tears pricking against her eyelids and she blinked them away.

Max trailed a finger along the shelf, in the manner of someone checking for dust. "So here's our little problem. Out of the blue, I have a niece, someone who deserves to carry the family name. I don't intend to run away from my responsibilities, such as they are, which means an investment of time as well as money, and please—" he held up one hand to cut off the heated protest forming on her lips "—spare me the aggrieved pride. As far as I can see it, everything has a solution and here's mine. My niece inherits the family name and so, on an incidental basis, do you. I'm proposing to marry you."

*Getting down to business
in the boardroom...and the bedroom!*

A secret romance, a forbidden affair,
a thrilling attraction...

What happens when two people work together
and simply can't help falling in love—
no matter how hard they try to resist?

Find out in our new series of stories
set against working backgrounds.

This month in

The Boss's Proposal by Cathy Williams

Since Vicky had started sleeping with her boss,
Max Forbes, she was worried he would discover
her secret. But when Max met the secret—
her young daughter, Chloe—he realized
immediately this was his late brother's child,
and insisted on marrying Vicky!

Cathy Williams

THE BOSS'S PROPOSAL

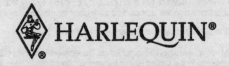

HARLEQUIN®

TORONTO • NEW YORK • LONDON
AMSTERDAM • PARIS • SYDNEY • HAMBURG
STOCKHOLM • ATHENS • TOKYO • MILAN • MADRID
PRAGUE • WARSAW • BUDAPEST • AUCKLAND

ISBN 0-373-12245-4

THE BOSS'S PROPOSAL

First North American Publication 2002.

CHAPTER ONE

'AH, YES, Miss Lockhart!' The severely coiffeured and immaculately suited middle aged woman who'd emerged from behind the smoked glass doors leading into the impressive foyer of Paxus PLC favoured her with a beaming smile. 'I'm Geraldine Hogg and I'm in charge of the typing pool.' She grasped Vicky's hand and shook it firmly. 'I have your application form here, my dear—' she waved the stapled papers at her '—and you're in for something of a surprise.'

At which, Vicky's heart sank. She didn't like surprises, and she hadn't spent half an hour battling with rush-hour traffic to find herself confronted with one. She'd applied for the post of typist at Paxus PLC because the pay offered was excellent and because working as a typist, whilst going nowhere career-wise, was just the sort of reliable job she needed while she got her house in order. Something undemanding which would give her the time she desperately needed to sort herself out.

'Now, my dear, why don't we go to my office and I'll explain all to you?' Geraldine Hogg had the sort of booming, hearty voice that Vicky associated with privately educated girls who had spent their school years getting their teeth into vigorous outdoor sports like hockey and netball. Her manner was brisk without being aggressive, and whatever so-called surprise lay ahead, Vicky felt that she would work well for the woman now ushering her through the smoked glass double doors and into a luxuriantly carpeted corridor flanked with offices.

'I must say, you seem rather over-qualified for the job advertised,' she said confidingly, and Vicky tried to suppress a sigh of disappointment.

'I make a very hard worker, Miss Hogg,' she ventured, half running to keep up with the enormous strides of the other woman.

She could feel her long, curly hair beginning to rebel against the clips she'd painstakingly used to restrain it and she nervously tried to shove it back into place with one hand, without missing a step. She needed this job and it wouldn't do to create the wrong impression, even though it was virtually impossible to look mature and sophisticated when her red-gold hair was congenitally disobedient and her expression, however hard she tried to look stern, was constantly ambushed by her freckles.

'Here we are!' Geraldine Hogg stopped abruptly in front of one of the doors and Vicky only just missed careering into the back of her. 'My typists are just through there.' She waved one sweeping hand at the large, open-planned area opposite her office, and Vicky peered into the room, imagining what it would be like to work there.

Her last job in Australia had been a far cry from this. There, she had been one of the personal assistants to the director of a sprawling public company.

'Come in, come in. Tea? Coffee?' She indicated a chair facing her desk and waited until Vicky had sat down before summoning a young girl through to bring them something to drink. 'I can recommend the coffee, my dear. None of this instant stuff.'

'Yes, fine, I'd love a cup,' Vicky said faintly. She felt as though she had been yanked along at dizzying speed so that she needed to recover her breath. 'White, no sugar. Thank you very much.'

'Now, I won't keep you,' Geraldine sat forward, both

elbows on the desk and gave her an intent stare. 'I'll just tell you about the little surprise I have in store for you!' She linked her fingers together and cocked her head to one side. 'First of all, let me say that I was highly impressed with your CV.' She glanced down at the highly impressive CV and flicked through it casually while Vicky's head whirled with all the dreadful permutations of this so-called surprise in store for her. 'Lots of qualifications!' She rattled off a few of them, which only served to emphasise how ridiculously over-qualified Vicky was for the job in question. 'You must have been quite an asset to the company you worked for!'

'I'd like to think so.' Vicky attempted a confident smile but was quietly glad for the interruption of the young girl bringing two cups of coffee.

'Why did you decide to leave Australia?' Sharp blue eyes scrutinised Vicky's face, but before Vicky could answer Geraldine held up one hand and said, 'No! No point answering that! I'll just fill you in on your position here. First of all, we feel that you would be wasted working as a typist...'

'Ah.' She could feel the sting of disappointed tears prick the back of her eyes. Since leaving Australia four months previously, Vicky had worked in various temporary jobs, none of which had been satisfactory, and the two permanent posts she'd applied for had both turned her down for the very reason Geraldine Hogg appeared to be giving her now. Unless she secured a proper job she would find herself running into financial problems, and she couldn't afford to start dipping into her meagre savings. Not in her situation.

'But, fortunately,' Geraldine swept on in a satisfied voice, 'we have something far better to interview you for, my dear, so there's no need for you to look quite so dejected. The head of our organisation will be spending a great deal more time in this particular subsidiary and he needs a secretary. Admittedly, you're a bit young for the post, but your qualifications provide a good argument for putting you forward for the job, which, incidentally, will pay double the one you were to be interviewed for!'

'Working for the head of the organisation?' From past experience Vicky knew that nothing came without a catch, and this opportunity sounded just a little too good to be true.

'I'll take you up to see him now, and while I don't, obviously, guarantee that the job is yours, your past experience will certainly stand in your favour.'

It occurred to Vicky that none of this was happening. It was all some bizarre dream which would end the minute she opened her eyes. In fact, applying to the company had had a dream-like feel about it from the start. She had seen the advertisement in the newspaper and the name of the company had triggered a memory somewhere in the dark recesses of her mind. Shaun, in one of his eternal, self-glorifying rambles, had mentioned it as one of the myriad companies his family owned and the name had stuck because it had been the name of the road on which she had lived with her aunt in Sydney. Just answering the advert had taken will-power, because Shaun was possibly the one person in the world whose memory made her recoil in revulsion. But answer it she had, partly through curiosity to see proof of the great Forbes Dynasty and partly because the pay offered had been too good to refuse.

Now, she curiously looked around her as she was shown up to the third floor. The décor was muted and luxuriant. The central areas were open plan but fringed with small, private offices, sheltered from prying eyes by the same smoked glass as in the foyer. The company—which, she recalled from the newspaper advert, had not been going for very long—had obviously chosen the nursery supplying its plants with some care, because in between the usual lush green artificial trees that most successful companies sported were expensive orchids and roses which couldn't be very easy to maintain.

'Hope you don't mind the walk up,' Geraldine was saying briskly at her side. 'I can't abide elevators. Much prefer a spot of good old-fashioned exercise. World would be a better place if people just got off their arses, pardon my French, and used their legs a bit more!'

Vicky, busy looking around her, puffed and panted an agreement. Somehow she found it difficult to associate Shaun with clean, efficient, seemingly well-run surroundings like these. She could feel her mind going down familiar paths and focused her attention on Geraldine and what she was saying, which appeared to be a congratulatory monologue on the massive and successful Forbes Holdings, of which Paxus PLC was a small but blossoming satellite. She wondered whether any mention would be made of Shaun, or even the brother, the one who lived in New York, but there was no mention of either in between the steady stream of growth, profit and share price chat.

''Course, I've worked for the family for twenty years now. Wanted a career teaching sport, but I did the back in, my dear, and ended up going along the secretarial road. Not that I've regretted a minute of working here,' she confided, and just when Vicky imagined that the bracing talk might become less factual and more personal, Geraldine paused in front of a door and knocked authoritatively.

'Yes!'

Mysteriously, Vicky saw that the plain, down-to-earth face had turned pink and, when Geraldine pushed open the door and poked her head in, her voice was almost kittenish.

'Miss Lockhart here for you, sir.'

'Who?'

'Miss Lockhart.'

'Now?'

Vicky gazed, embarrassed, at the unappealing abstract painting on the wall opposite. Was this 'surprise' job offer also a surprise to the man in question, or were heads of organisations exempt from good manners?

'I did inform you a week ago…' Geraldine said, lapsing into her more autocratic voice.

'Show her in, Gerry, show her in.' At which, Geraldine pushed open the door wider and stepped back to allow Vicky through.

The man was sitting behind a huge desk, lounging in a black leather swivel chair which he had pushed away from the desk so that he could cross his legs in comfort.

Under the rapid pounding of her heart, Vicky was dimly aware of the door gently being shut behind her, and then she was left, stranded, in the middle of the large office, like a fish that had suddenly found itself floundering in the middle of a desert. Her breathing was laboured and she hardly dared move a muscle, because if she did she suspected that her shaky legs would collapse completely.

All she could see was the nightmare in front of her. The dark hair, the strong angular face, those peculiar grey eyes.

'Are you all right, Miss Lockhart?' The question was posed in an impatient voice from which could be dredged not even passing concern. 'You look as though you're about to faint and I really haven't got the time to deal with a fainting secretary.'

'I'm fine. Thank you.' Fine, she thought, considering the shock that had rocked her to the foundations. She was still standing, wasn't she? If that wasn't fine, what was?

'Then sit down.' He nodded curtly at the chair facing

him. 'I'm afraid it slipped my mind that you were supposed to be coming today... Your application form's somewhere here...bear with me for a moment...'

'That's fine!' Suddenly Vicky found her voice. 'In fact, there's no need to waste your time interviewing me. I don't think I would be suitable at all for this job.'

She just wanted to get out of the office and out of the building as fast as her legs could take her. Her skin was on fire and her temples were beginning to pound.

He didn't immediately answer. Instead, he paused in his search for the elusive CV and the pale grey eyes became suddenly watchful as they scanned her flushed face.

'Oh, really?' he said slowly. 'And why do you think that would be?' He stood up. A towering, well-built man, he strolled to the bay window behind his chair, from where he perched against the ledge, all the better to watch her.

Between the host of emotions and thoughts besieging her, Vicky tried to locate a functioning part of her brain which might come up with a good excuse for showing up at this company for a job, only to spuriously announce that she had to leave immediately. Nothing was forthcoming.

'You know, you *do* look a little nervous.' He brushed his chin reflectively with one finger while continuing to scrutinise her face with the lazy intensity of a predator eyeing up potential prey. 'Not one of these highly strung, neurotic types, are you?'

'Yes,' Vicky agreed, ready to clutch any lifeline offered that might get her out of the place, 'highly strung and very neurotic. No use to a man like you.'

'A man like me? And what kind of man might that be?'

Vicky dropped her eyes rather than reveal the answer to that particular question. The strength of the response she would give him might just blow him off his feet.

'Sit down, why don't you? You're beginning to interest

me, Miss Lockhart.' He waited until she had made her way
to the chair and flopped down, then allowed a few more
seconds to pass, during which he looked at her as though
trying to unravel the workings of her mind.

'Now, tell me why I'm beginning to feel that there's
something going on here that I know nothing about.'

'I don't know what you mean.'

'I'll let that pass.' He flashed her smile that indicated
that the subject had been dropped but by no means abandoned.

*He has a God complex, the bastard. He's always felt
that he could run my life, along with everyone else's.* She
could hear Shaun's voice, high and resentful as it always
had been whenever he spoke about his brother. Vicky's
tightly controlled mind slowly began to unravel as her eyes
locked with Max Hedley Forbes. Because that was his
name. She'd heard it often enough from Shaun's lips. A
litany of bitterness and antagonism towards a brother
whose mission in life, she'd been told often enough, had
been to undermine as many people as he could in the min-
imum amount of time. He'd been a monster of selfishness,
Shaun had said to her, a man who only knew how to take,
a man who rode roughshod over the rest of the human race
and most of all over his one and only brother, whose name
he'd discredited so thoroughly that even his father had
chosen to turn his back on his son.

It had never occurred to her when she applied for this
job that fate would be waiting for her just around the corner. Max Forbes lived in New York and had done for
years. She'd never thought that she would end up finding
him in an office building in Warwick, of all places. The
past squeezed her soul and she briefly closed her eyes,
giving in to the vertigo threatening to overwhelm her.

Shaun might have turned out to be a nightmare, but

nightmares were not born, they were made. The world and the people in it had shaped him, and the man coolly inspecting her now had been pivotal in the shaping of his brother. However awful Shaun had been, wasn't this man opposite her worse?

'So,' the dark, velvety voice drawled, dragging her away from her painful trip down memory lane and back to the present, 'you claim to be neurotic and highly strung, yet—' he reached forward to a stack of papers on the desk and extracted one, from which he read '—you still managed to sustain a reasonably high-powered job in Australia from which you left with glowing recommendations. Odd, wouldn't you agree? Or perhaps your neuroses were under control at that point in time?'

Vicky refrained from comment and instead contented herself with staring out of the window, which offered a view of sky and red-brick buildings.

'Has Geraldine given you any indication as to why this post has become available?' He moved around the desk and perched on it, so that he was directly facing Vicky, looking down at her.

'Not in any great detail, no,' Vicky told him, 'but honestly, there's no point launching into any explanations. The fact of the matter is...' What was the fact of the matter? 'The fact of the matter is that I had really set my heart on working in a typing pool...'

His lips twitched, but when he answered his voice was serious and considering.

'Of course. I quite understand that you might not want to compromise your undoubted talents by getting a good job with career prospects...'

Vicky shot him a brief look from under thick, dark lashes, momentarily disconcerted by the suggestion of humour beneath the sarcasm. 'I have an awful lot on my plate just now,' she said vaguely. 'I wouldn't want to take on anything demanding because I don't think that I would be able to do it justice.'

'What?'

'I beg your pardon?'

'*What* have you got on your plate?' His eyes scanned her CV then focused on her.

'Well,' Vicky stuttered, taken aback by the directness of the question, 'I've only recently returned from Australia and I have a lot of things to do concerning…my house and generally settling in…' This explanation skirted so broadly around the truth that she could feel the colour rise to her cheeks.

'Why did you decide to go to Australia?'

'My mother…passed away…I felt that the change would do me good…and I just happened to stay a great deal longer than I had anticipated. I landed a job in a very good company quite early on and I was promoted in the first six months. I…it was easier than coming back to England and dealing with…'

'Your loss?'

Vicky stiffened at the perceptiveness behind the question. She'd once considered Shaun to be a perceptive, sensitive person. Perhaps illusions along those lines ran in the Forbes family.

'I would appreciate it if we could terminate this interview now.' She began getting to her feet, smoothing down the dark grey skirt, nervously brushing non-existent flecks of dust from it rather than face those amazing, unsettling grey eyes. 'I'm sorry if I've wasted your time. I realise that you're a very busy man, and time is money. Had I been aware of the situation, I would have telephoned to cancel the appointment. As I said, I'm not interested in a job that's going to monopolise my free time.'

'Your references,' he said coolly, ignoring her pointed attempt to leave his office, 'from the Houghton Corporation are glowing...' He looked at her carefully while she remained in dithering uncertainty on her feet, unable to turn her back and walk out of the office but reluctant to sit back down and allow him to think that the job in question was open for debate. 'Very impressive, and all the more so because I know James Houghton very well.'

'You *know* him?' Several potential catastrophes presented themselves to her when she heard this and she weakly sat back down. It wouldn't do for Max Forbes to contact her old boss in Australia. There were too many secrets hidden away there, secrets she had no intention of disclosing.

'We went to school together a million years ago.' He pushed himself up from the desk and began prowling around the room, one minute within her line of vision, the next a disembodied voice somewhere behind her. If his tactic was to unsettle her, then he was going about it the right way. 'He's a good businessman. A recommendation from him counts for a hell of a lot.' He paused and the silence from behind her made the hairs on the back of her neck stand on end. 'Where in Australia did you live?'

'In the city. My aunt has a house there.' There was an element of danger in this line of questioning but Vicky had no idea how to retrieve the situation.

'Did much socialising?'

'With whom?' she asked cautiously. It would help, she thought, if he would return within her line of vision so that she could see the expression on his face—but then, on reflection, perhaps it wasn't a bad thing that she couldn't. After all, he would be able to see hers, and she had a great deal more to hide than he would ever have imagined in a million years.

'People from your work.' She could sense him as he walked slowly round to the side of her. His presence made her feel clammy and claustrophobic. Out of the corner of her eye, she could make him out as he lounged against the wall, hands shoved deep into his trouser pockets, head tilted slightly to one side as though carefully weighing up what she was saying. Weighing it up and, she thought with a flash of sudden foreboding, storing up every word to be used at a later date in evidence against her.

Not that there would *be* a later date, she reminded herself. Powerful though he was, he couldn't compel her to work for his company. He might grill her now because she had been stupid enough to make him think that there was more to her than met the eye, but very shortly she would be gone and he would be nothing more than a freakish reminder of how eerie coincidence could be. The thought of imminent escape steadied her nerves and she even managed to force a smile to her face.

'Off and on. I had a lot of friends in Sydney. The Australians are a very friendly lot.' She risked a sideways glance at him.

'So I've been told. My brother certainly thought so.'

'You had a brother out there?' A slow crawl of treacherous colour stole across her face and she could feel a fine perspiration begin to film above her lip.

'Shaun Forbes.' He allowed the name to register. 'My twin.'

He had never told her. She'd known Shaun for nearly a year and a half and he'd never once mentioned that the brother whose name he reviled was his identical twin. She imagined now that it must have been deeply galling to have so spectacularly failed to live up to a brother who had emerged from the womb at the same time as he had and had been given exactly the same upbringing and privileges, yet had succeeded.

Seeing Max Forbes had been a heart-stopping shock. There was enough in their physical make-up to send her spinning sickeningly back into the past and every memory she had spent so long trying to crush had reared their ugly heads with gleeful malice.

'He was quite prominent on the social scene, I gather.' His mouth twisted and he turned away and strode towards the desk.

'No. The name doesn't ring a bell.' The words almost got stuck in her throat. This was what it felt like to be toyed with by the devil, she thought. Life had not been easy since she'd returned to England. The last batch of tenants to occupy her mother's house had been cavalier in their treatment of it and, frustratingly, the estate agents who handled the rental had had nothing to say on the subject. So, on top of the uphill task of finding work and getting her finances straight, there was the little problem of the house, which needed a complete overhaul. Even the walls seemed to smell.

And then there was Chloe.

Vicky half closed her eyes and a wave of nausea rushed through her.

'I'm surprised. James spent a lot of time in his company. I might have expected that you would have seen him at some point in the offices.'

Vicky, whose vocal cords were failing to co-operate with her brain, shook her head and looked blankly at the man staring at her.

'No?' he prodded, glancing back down at her CV, and she made an inarticulate, choking sound by way of reply.

'Well, perhaps not. Shaun probably wouldn't have noticed you, anyway.'

That succeeded in clearing her head admirably. He surely couldn't have meant to insult her, but insult her he had. If only he knew that seek her out was precisely what his hideous brother had done. Charmed her with his smooth conversation and his offerings of flowers and empty flattery. Told her that she was destined to rescue him from himself, thanked her with tears in his eyes for making him want to be a better human being. And she'd fallen for all the claptrap—hook, line and sinker. It hadn't taken long before the mask had begun to disintegrate and she'd begun to see the ugliness behind the charming façade.

'Thank you very much,' she said coldly.

'Why did you decide to leave Australia if you had such a brilliant job and hectic social life?'

The question was irrelevant, considering she had no intention of working for the man, but fear of arousing yet more of his curiosity restrained her from telling him to mind his own business.

'I never intended to build my life out there. I felt that it was time to come back to England.'

Chloe. Everything had centred around Chloe.

'And you've had temp jobs since returning? The pay's pretty poor, wouldn't you agree?'

'I get by.' Lousy was the word for it.

'And you're living—?' For a minute, the piercing grey eyes left her face and perused the paper in front of him. '—just outside Warwick...rented place?'

'My mother left her house to me when she...died. It's been rented out for the past few years.'

He shoved the paper away from him, leaned back in his

chair with his hands folded behind his head and looked at her without bothering to disguise his curiosity.

'Young woman, who's just returned from abroad, and doubtless wants to refurnish house, rejects job that is vastly superior to the one for which she originally applied. Help me out there with a logical explanation? If there's one thing I can't stand, it's a mystery. I always feel that mysteries are there to be solved, and, by hook or by crook, guess what...?'

'What?' Vicky asked, mesmerised by his eyes. When she'd first met Shaun, the first thing she'd noticed had been his eyes. Those pale eyes and black hair and the chiselled, beautiful lines of his face. He was like an Adonis. If she'd had any sense, she would have seen past the outside to the man within and it wouldn't have taken her long to notice the weakness behind the good looks, the restless feverish energy of a man who needed to find his fixes outside himself, the mouth that could thin to a cruel line in a matter of seconds.

With that in mind, it sickened her that she could feel something inside her tighten alarmingly at the sight of his twin.

'I always get to the bottom of them.' He gave her a slow, dangerous smile and she shivered.

Max Forbes was so like his brother, and yet so dissimilar in ways that she couldn't quite put her finger on. If Shaun's looks had captivated because of their prettiness, his brother's hypnotised because of their power, and if Shaun had always known what to say to get the girls into bed, Vicky imagined that his brother achieved what he wanted by the very fact that he disregarded the normal little social conventions and said precisely what he wanted, despite the consequences. He had the sort of rugged, I'll-do-as-I-damn-well-want charisma that women, she suspected, would find difficult to resist. Even Geraldine Hogg had become coy in his presence.

Max Forbes looked at the small figure on the chair. She looked more like a child than a woman, with that pointed elfin face and pale, freckled skin. The picture of innocence. But his instincts were telling a different story. Something was not quite above board and his desire to find out *what* surprised him. He hadn't felt so damned *curious* about anyone for a long time. He stared at her and felt a rush of satisfied pleasure when she blushed and looked away quickly.

Oh, yes. Life had ceased to be merely an affair of making money and making love, both with a great deal of flair and, lately, not much pleasure or satisfaction. Vicky Lockhart had something to hide and the thought of discovering what sent a ripple of enjoyment through him. It was a sensation so alien that it took him a few seconds to recognise what it was.

'Oh, how very interesting,' she said politely, her brown eyes widening. The sun, streaming through the window, caught her hair and seemed to turn it to flames.

It was, he thought, a most unusual shade of red, and, connoisseur that he was, he was almost certain that it hadn't come out of a bottle. Of course, she wasn't his type. Not at all. He'd always gone for tall, full-breasted women, but still, he felt his mind wander as he imagined what that hair would look like, were it not pulled back. How long was it? Long, he imagined. Long and unruly. Nothing at all like the sleek-haired women he dated. Did the hair, he wondered, match the personality? Underneath that sweet, childish façade was there a hot, steamy, untamed woman bursting to get out? He smiled at the passing thought and was startled to find that his body had responded rather too vigorously to the image he'd mentally conjured up. Getting aroused like this made him feel like an adolescent, and he cleared his throat in a business-like fashion.

'I don't know if Geraldine mentioned the pay...' He waited for her curiosity to take the bait, then he rattled off a sum that was roughly twice what he'd had in mind for the job in question. He could see the glimmer of interest illuminate the brown eyes and her small fists clenched at the sides of the chair as though she had to steady herself.

'That's a very generous salary. She did mention that the pay would be more than the job advertised in the newspaper...'

She wanted to accept. He could see it written on her face and he waited patiently for her to nod her head.

'But, really, I'm afraid I must say no.'

It took a few seconds for that to sink in.

'What?' Not much floored him, but for a passing moment he could feel himself rendered speechless.

'I can't accept.'

He looked at the small, elfin face, the delicate mouth, the soft brown eyes fringed with impossibly long auburn lashes, and was assailed by a humiliating sensation of powerlessness. He couldn't *make* her accept his offer—he wasn't even that sure *why* he was so infuriated by her refusal; he just knew that he wanted to shake her until she agreed to work for him. The absurdity of his reaction was enough to make him shake his head and smile. He must be losing his mind. Wrapping up New York and then moving to the UK must have conspired to bring about some kind of subliminal breakdown, or else why would he now be staring at a perfect stranger and feeling this way?

He glanced down at the desk and began drumming his pen on it.

'Of course, if I can't persuade you...'

'I'm flattered that you've been prepared to try...' She stood up and gave him an awkward and, he was irritated to see, relieved smile.

'Thousands of people would kill for the job offer I've just made you.' He heard his over-hearty voice and bared his teeth in a smile of good-mannered regret. His eyes flicked to her face and he could feel himself stiffen once again at the thought of what she would look like with her hair down. Then, to his utter disgust, and completing his inexorable decline into pubescent irrationality, he glanced down at her breasts, two small bumps underneath the bulk of shirt and jacket, and wondered what they would be like. Tiny, he imagined. Small, pointed, freckled with rosy nipples. Red hair tumbling down a naked body and rose-peaked breasts just big enough to fit into his...

He virtually gulped and was obliged, as he stood up, to conceal his treacherous body by leaning forward on the desk and supporting himself on his hands.

'Are you quite sure you won't reconsider...?'

'Quite sure.' She looked at him uncertainly, then stretched out her hand, which he took and shook, paying lip service to good manners. He could tell that even that small gesture was not one she particularly wanted to make but courtesy had compelled her.

What was her story?

He made her nervous, but *why*? He didn't threaten her...or did he? He wondered whether they'd met before, but he was sure that he would have remembered. There was something unforgettable about the ethereal delicacy of that face and the teasing disarray of that remarkable hair. She *had* been to Australia, however...

'If I speak to James, I shall mention I've met you,' he murmured, walking her to the door and he felt the momentary pause in her steps.

'Of course. And do you…keep in regular touch with him?'

'I used to. He occasionally kept an eye on my wayward brother.'

'And he no longer does?'

He picked up the struggle in her voice with interest.

'My brother died a while back in a car crash, Miss Lockhart.'

Vicky nodded, and instead of proffering the usual mutterings of sympathy rested her hand on the door knob and turned it, ready to flee. She knew that she should express some kind of courteous regret at that, but honesty stopped her from doing so. She had no regrets at Shaun's fate. To forgive was divine, but it wasn't human, and she had no aspirations to divinity.

'Well, perhaps we'll meet again.' *Perhaps, indeed. Much sooner than you think.*

'I doubt it.' She smiled and pulled open the door. 'But thanks for the job offer, anyway. And good luck in finding someone for the post.'

CHAPTER TWO

THE GARDEN had been the most distressing sight to greet her upon her return to England and to the modest three-bedroom cottage that had been her mother's. She'd more or less expected to find the house in something of a state. It had seen a variety of tenants, not all of them reliable family units, and even when her mother had been alive it had been in dire need of repair. But the garden had broken her heart. A combination of young children, cigarette-smoking teenagers and, from the looks of things, adults with hobnailed boots had rendered it virtually unrecognisable.

One more thing, she thought wearily, to bring to the attention of the agency that had handled the letting, although what precisely the point of doing that would be, she had no idea. Marsha, the woman in whose hands Vicky had hurriedly but confidently left the house, had left the firm eighteen months back, and since then the house had been handled by a series of people, none of whom had done justice to it. Perhaps they'd thought that she would never return to England, or at least not quite as unexpectedly as she had in the end.

It broke her heart to think of all the time and effort that her mother had spent in the small, immaculate garden. A decade ago, it had been her salvation after the death of her husband, Vicky's father, and it had steadfastly seen her through her ups and downs, providing comfort and soothing her when her illness took hold and she no longer had the energy to go walking or attempt anything energetic.

24

She'd laid borders and hedgerows and planted wild roses and shrubbery with the imagination of someone whose every other outlet had been prematurely barred. Vicky could remember the summer evenings spent out in it, listening to the sounds of nature and appreciating the tumult of colour.

The cottage was set back at the end of a lane in a part of Warwickshire noted for its rural beauty. The small garden, now sporting an interesting array of weeds which formed a charming tangle around the occasional outcrop of lager bottles, ambled down to a white fence, beyond which stretched cultivated fields. A plot of reasonably well-maintained land bordered by trees separated the cottage from its neighbour, a rather more substantial family house to the right. To the left woodland kept the well-used roads at bay.

Vicky, sweating in her layers of clothing and grimy with the exertions of her Saturday morning garden clear-out, peered through some bush at yet another aluminium can. Robert 'call-me-Robbie' at the agency had assured her that whatever she'd found in the garden had not been there when the house and grounds had been inspected, and she knew, anyway, that she was pretty late to be lodging complaints about the state of the garden. Only recently had she managed to find the time to do anything other than superficially maintain it, a thirty-minute job whenever she found the time to spare.

This was the first time she'd really got stuck in, and that only because she'd managed to farm Chloe out to one of her playmates from school.

The thought of her five-year-old daughter automatically brought a smile to her lips.

At least she had no worries on that front. Chloe had

taken to the school and her classmates like a duck to water and that had been an enormous source of relief.

She stuck on her gardening glove, wriggled her hand into the undergrowth, half her mind still playing with the thought of her gorgeous raven-haired daughter, so different physically from her, and the other half preoccupied with the unwelcome thought that she might find one or two bugs in addition to the can, and was about to reach for the offending object when a voice said from behind her,

'Thought I might find you here. Hope I'm not interrupting anything.'

The shock of the voice sent her falling face-first into the bush, and when she emerged, after a short struggle with greenery, earth and some unfortunate spiky things, she was decidedly the worse for wear.

'What are *you* doing here?' She hadn't even rescued the can!

Max Forbes, in the bracing winter sunshine, looked horribly, impossibly *good*. The brisk wind had ruffled his dark hair so that it sprang away from his face in an endearingly boyish way that was at odds with the powerful angularity of his features, and as his trench coat blew open she spotted a casual attire of dark trousers and a thick cream jumper with a pale-coloured shirt underneath. The shock of seeing him in her garden and the impact of his presence made her take a couple of steps back.

'Be careful you don't fall into the bush again.'

'*What* are you doing here?' Now that her slow-witted brain had come to terms with his looming great masculine presence, her thought patterns suddenly shot into fifth gear, and the realisation that Chloe was out for the morning was enough to render her weak-kneed with relief.

'Actually, I've just come from your neighbours down

the road. Small world, wouldn't you say? Thompsons. Live three houses away.'

'I don't know the names of the people here, aside from the elderly couple opposite.'

'So I thought I'd drop in, see whether you'd managed to find yourself a job as yet.'

Standing opposite him, head tilted at an awkward angle because without heels she was a good ten inches shorter than him, Vicky felt small, grubby and disadvantaged. The long braid hanging down her back was an insult to anyone with a sense of style and there was mud and soil all over her face, clothes, hands—probably in her hair as well. Her sturdy wellingtons were covered in muck. When she removed the gardening gloves, she would doubtless find that they matched the state of her nails.

'It's only been three days and no luck yet. Thank you.' She refused to budge even though the cold was seeping through her jumper and waxed jacket and making her shiver. She stuck her hands in the pockets of the jacket and glared at him.

'Too bad.'

'I'm sure something will turn up.'

'Oh, I don't know. Jobs in typing pools are thin on the ground. 'Course, you'll have no trouble getting something much better paid with infinitely more prospects, but who needs *that* sort of work?'

There was a veiled amusement in his voice that only made her more addled and crosser than she already was.

'Look, why don't we go inside? I've got time for a cup of tea and you can tell me all about Australia.'

'There's nothing to tell.' A telltale pulse was beating rhythmically in the hollow of her neck and the little bud of panic that had begun to sprout the minute she'd heard his voice flowered into full bloom.

They couldn't possibly go inside. Chloe wasn't around, but signs of her were everywhere. He didn't know that she had a child and that was the way she intended it to remain. It had been the only piece of sheer luck since meeting him. She'd answered the advertisement and had sheepishly omitted to mention Chloe simply because she had gleaned from several sources that a child in the background prompted awkward questions about childcare and being a single parent; this was the road to certain rejection by any company. School and Betsy, the lady who helped her out in the evenings sometimes, meant that there were no problems on the childcare front, and she reckoned, naively, that if she ever got offered a job she would inform her employers at that point and hope that they would take her on the strength of her interview, even once they knew of Chloe's existence.

Max looked down at her and confusingly wanted to do a number of things at the same time. First, he wanted to clear out, because he had no idea what had possessed him to go there in the first place. Unfortunately, and much to his immense frustration, he also wanted to stay put, because seeing her again had somehow managed to render him even more intrigued than he'd been on their first encounter. He also wanted to brush some of that dirt off her face, if only to see what her reaction would be. In fact, the urge to do just that was so powerful that he clasped his hands behind his back and purposely looked away.

'Actually, I haven't just dropped by,' he said eventually, resenting her for putting him in a position where he was about to embark on an out-and-out lie and resenting himself for his own pathetic weakness that had brought him here to start with.

'Oh, no?' she asked warily.

'It's to do with your house, as a matter of fact.'

'What? What's to do with my house?'

'Why don't we go inside and talk about it?' He didn't think that he had ever been so bloody underhanded in his life before, and all because he hadn't been able to get this chit of a girl out of his head. She had fired up his interest, for reasons he couldn't fathom, and now here he was, behaving like some shady character in a third-rate movie. He had never, *but never*, done anything remotely like this in *his entire life* because of a woman, and he could hardly believe that he was doing it now. Conniving like a two-bit criminal.

She didn't say anything. Instead, she headed towards the house, leaning forward into the wind, which looked as though it might just lift her off her feet and sweep her away if she wasn't careful. Max followed behind by a few paces, his teeth clenched in exasperation as she told him to wait outside until she'd tidied herself up.

He raised his eyebrows in amusement. 'Why outside?'

'Because,' Vicky said coldly, 'it's my house and that's what I'm telling you to do.' Upon which she promptly shut the door in his face before he could open his mouth to protest further.

She had never moved with more speed. The house was thankfully clean, and in under three minutes she'd managed to stash away all evidence of her daughter. It took her a further five minutes to sling off the grubby clothes and replace them with a pair of faded jeans and a long-sleeved striped jumper that had seen better days. The hair would have to remain in its charming grass-ridden style.

'So,' she said, yanking open the door to surprise him leaning against it, 'what about my house?'

'Has anyone ever mentioned to you that you are completely eccentric?'

'No.' She led the way into the sitting room, which had been the first room in the house to undergo redecoration and was now in restful greens and creams and blessedly free of childish clutter. She glanced at her watch and saw that it was at least another two hours before Chloe was dropped back to the house. More than enough time to get rid of Max Forbes, whose presence was enough to bring her out in a cold sweat.

'My house,' she reminded him bluntly, once she had installed him in a chair. 'I won't sit,' she said. 'I feel filthy. Now, what about my house?'

'I can't conduct a conversation like this.' He shook his head and stood up. 'Which is a shame because I think you'd be very interested in what I have to say, but if your ill manners override your self-interest, then—' he shrugged eloquently '—at least I tried…'

Vicky looked at him doubtfully. He really shouldn't be here at all, and she knew that she should just throw him out. In fact, she should never have let him in in the first place. Hadn't this been the same old story with his brother? From the minute she'd set eyes on him, she'd known that he was bad news. He'd been too good-looking, too smooth-talking and too well connected to be interested in a girl like her, but he'd stopped at her desk where she'd been working with her head down and he'd leaned over just enough for her to feel overpowered by him. Everything she'd said, even *Please go away, I really must get on with my work* had seemed to amuse him, and he had had a way of laughing deep in his throat, a sexy laugh, while his eyes never left her face, that had made her feel uncomfortable and excited at the same time.

So if Shaun had achieved that with her, then how much

more dangerous was his brother, who had struck her as being leagues ahead of him? And if her own need to protect herself wasn't sufficient to keep her away from Max Forbes, then what about her daughter?

Dark-haired, grey-eyed, Chloe had been the spitting image of Shaun from the day of her birth. There was no way under the sun she could have been anything but a Forbes, and time had strengthened rather than lessened the resemblance.

If only theirs had been the tried and tested failed romance. If only Shaun had done the decent thing and walked away from her and his baby so that they could live their lives in peace. But, like all weak men, Shaun had needed his punch bag, and she had been his. He had rarely raised his hand to her, and then only under the influence of drink or drugs, but he hadn't needed to go down that road to gain her compliance. All he'd had to do was threaten to take Chloe away from her. It had suited him to pretend to the world that he had never fathered a child, but he'd always taken great satisfaction in reminding her in private that if his family ever discovered his progeny then they would move in to claim what they would feel was rightfully theirs. Especially, he'd been fond of saying, if they could see the uncanny resemblance she bore to the Forbes clan.

So, however painful it was to her, she'd lived in the shadow of fear. Sometimes days would pass, weeks even, and there would be no sign of him. Then he would return and demand his sexual privileges—and she had slept with him and wept bitter tears afterwards.

To have Max Forbes under her roof was to have Lucifer with the key to her front door. She'd heard enough about him to know that the existence of Chloe would be of great interest to him. Would he try and spirit her away, or take her through the courts for custody? Ninety-nine point nine per cent of her knew that her child was safe, but that nought point one per cent was enough to terrify.

She'd spent years protecting her daughter from an abusive man. She'd watched in helpless fear as he'd wielded his power over them both, smilingly and ruthlessly intimidating. Vicky had lived on a knife's edge, waiting in dreaded expectation of the worst. Now, Vicky knew she must keep Chloe's existence a secret from Max. For all she knew, these brothers might have more in common than mere appearance. Much more. And she had not escaped from one destructive cycle only to find herself hooked into another. She would never give a man that power over her again. Never.

Max was standing by the door, saying something, and Vicky's attention snapped back to the present. The house. She couldn't afford to run into problems with the house. She had barely begun to find her feet and Chloe could do without any more changes in her life.

'Sit down. Please. I might as well hear what you have to say.' She nodded to the chair which he had just vacated and he appeared to give her request some thought.

'You seem to act as though *I'm* doing *you* a favour. I assure you, Miss Lockhart, you couldn't be further from the truth.'

'I'm sorry. I have…things on my mind.'

'Why don't you go and change? Clean clothes might improve your temper.'

She frowned and looked very much as though she would have liked to argue that particular point with him, but instead she informed him that she would bring him a cup of tea, or coffee.

That, she thought, should keep him anchored in one place. The last thing she needed was Max Forbes prowling through her house. At least the sitting room—the one place that was kept neat at all times, even if the rest of the cottage was in a state of disarray—contained relatively few personal bits and pieces. She'd stuffed the pictures of Chloe in the weather-beaten pine trunk behind the sofa, and the books that lined the bookshelf on either side of the fireplace were the sort of everyday reading that gave nothing away. The ornaments had mostly belonged to her mother and had been retrieved from the attic where they had been stored while the house had been rented out. It was true what they said about there being safety in anonymity.

When she returned to the sitting room with a mug of tea, it was to find him innocently perusing the newspaper which had been lying on the low, square battered pine table in front of the fireplace. She almost said *Good*, but managed to resist the temptation.

'I won't be a moment,' she told him stiffly, and, just in case he got any ideas about exploring the place, she firmly shut the sitting room door behind her. Then she looked at her watch, to make sure that time was still on her side.

Showering and changing took a matter of fifteen minutes. Self-beautification, even if the situation demanded it, was something she rarely did. Now, she just changed into a clean pair of jeans, a clean T-shirt and re-braided her hair without going to the bother of combing out all the knots, of which there would be thousands. Later, she would wash and shampoo her hair.

'Now,' she said, slipping into the room and seeing, with relief, that he was still absorbed in the newspaper, 'you were going to tell me about my house.'

'Have you heard the rumours?'

'What rumours?'

'About the supermarket. Perhaps I should say *hyper-*

market, because apparently there'll be parking for hundreds of cars. If not thousands.'

Vicky, sitting cross-legged on the large comfy chair facing him, looked at him in horror. For a minute, she actually forgot that she was supposed to be on guard. She leaned forward, elbows on thighs, mouth open.

'You're joking.'

'Horrendous, isn't it? I can't bear those sprawling supermarkets myself. I much prefer smaller, more personal places to shop. Between Fortnum and Mason's and Harrods, I've never had a problem finding what I want. Tell me, is there an equivalent here, by any chance?' Now that he had launched into his lie, he couldn't wait to distance himself from it. He glanced at her face and discovered that he couldn't tear his eyes away. Her mouth was slightly parted and sitting like that, all folded into the chair in a way he had never seen a woman do before, she looked even more appealingly vulnerable. The T-shirt was small and close fitting and lovingly outlined her small, rounded breasts. He had to remind himself that he was only there because she had posed a mystery and he hated mysteries, and not because he was attracted to her, even though his mind kept churning up some embarrassingly graphic images of her body, unencumbered by clothing.

Frustratingly, she seemed to have no interest in him whatsoever. As a man who was accustomed to women looking at him, uninterest was proving to be a powerful aphrodisiac.

'Who told you this?' she asked, after a few seconds of shocked silence.

'No one and everyone. You know how it is with rumours. No one will admit to being the one who starts it. I mean, it may be entirely without foundation and certainly, in the business I'm in, I'm sure I would have *seen* something, something rather more substantial than gossip, but—' he sighed, reluctantly focusing his attention on the bookshelf behind her '—I feel better about telling you.'

'My house won't be worth a thing if a supermarket goes up opposite!' Vicky burst out on the verge of tears. 'Not that I want to sell up, but...'

'I'm sure it's all a load of tosh,' Max said hurriedly, guiltily seeing the sheen in her eyes.

'What if it's not?' She couldn't help herself. A supermarket! No, a *hypermarket*, with parking for ten thousand cars! It was the last straw. She blinked and, of its own accord, a tear trickled down her face. Her reaction appalled and dismayed her, but there seemed nothing she could do to stifle the ridiculous leakage.

She was hardly aware of what was happening until she felt Max perch on the wide upholstered arm of the chair and he dabbed the handkerchief at her face. With a groan of despair, Vicky took it from him and did a better job of mopping herself up, then she leant her head back and closed her eyes with a deep sigh.

'Look, I should never have said what I did.' Little did she know, he thought, how sincerely he meant that. He reached out and stroked some hair away from her face, then carried on stroking her damp cheeks. Her skin was like satin and, up close, her freckles made a fascinating pattern across the bridge of her nose. His thumb slid a bit further down and, finding no deterrent, lightly brushed her mouth.

'No, it's just as well to be prepared.' She opened her eyes and looked at him. There was a gentleness in his eyes that was unexpected enough to make the breath catch in her throat.

'I could find out easily enough whether there's truth behind the rumour,' he told her softly, feeling himself

harden as he carried on stroking her face. The woman was
an enigma. He could hardly remember why he thought that
she was hiding something. Right now, she was no more
than a vulnerable girl and she was bringing out all sorts
of ridiculously protective feelings he'd never known he
possessed.

'Could you?' she asked urgently, her eyes flicking
across his face. 'Do you think you could? It would mean
a great deal to me.' In the brief silence, she became aware
of his fingers on her face and she sprang away, pressing
herself back into the chair and looking at him.

'I could,' he said. He strolled back to his chair and
crossed his legs, then he slowly looked around him, as
though taking in his surroundings for the first time. 'You
know, I can't remember whether I mentioned this at the
interview, but I could arrange to have building work done
on this cottage at a nominal cost. The roof looks as though
it could do with an overhaul and your fireplace is going.'

'But I don't work for you.' She paused and looked at
him, while her hand idly rubbed her ankle tucked up on
the chair. 'I don't understand why you're so keen to hire
me.' There was genuine curiosity behind the question. *She*
knew why she couldn't accept his offer of a job, but she
had no idea why he'd continued to try and persuade her,
even when it was patently obvious that she wasn't interested.

Max sighed a long, resigned sigh and watched her from
under his lashes. He could still feel the softness of her skin
under his. 'I'm desperate. That's the bottom line. I've been
here for seven months during which time I've had a series
of temps, none of whom seemed capable of thinking on
their feet, and none of the applicants for the job on a permanent basis were suitable.'

'*None* of them?'

'That's right,' he said a little irritably, because there was an element of incredulous accusation in her voice that implied some kind of fault on his part.

'What was wrong with all of them?'

'Pretty much a combination of everything, actually.'

'Perhaps you're a bit too demanding,' Vicky volunteered helpfully, and her suggestion was met with a frown of instant and instinctive denial.

'I'm the least demanding boss I know. All I ask is a certain amount of initiative and common sense, along with the ability to do the usual things.'

'And how do you know *I* would have possessed the right qualities?' For the very briefest of moments, she put aside her fears of the man sitting opposite her and she could feel his personality working on her. In a minute, she told herself, she would put her defences back in place, but right now a rush of simple gratitude towards him had mellowed her. She found herself watching him intently, noticing, as she did so, how huge the differences were between him and Shaun, even though, at first glance, she'd been bowled over by their similarities. His face, she realised, was stronger, and stamped with lines of humour that had been missing from his brother's. His mouth was fuller, or perhaps that was just an optical illusion born of the fact that he just seemed more in command and more quietly self-assured than his brother. He lacked the ready smile that spoke of self-obsession and the carefully groomed look of someone to whom appearances were everything. In fact, the harder she stared at him, the less he seemed to resemble Shaun.

'Because you worked successfully for a man I have long respected,' he said simply. 'Aside from that, my first impression was favourable and I'm rarely wrong when it comes to first impressions.'

'Well, you should be,' Vicky heard herself say, her voice laced with creeping bitterness. She looked away and began toying with the end of her braid, flicking it back and forth, aware that two spots of burning colour had appeared on her cheeks.

Now, he thought, was not the time to probe deeper into that enigmatic little remark. She wasn't looking at him, in itself significant, but he could tell by the sudden flare of colour into her pale face that her reply had been instinctive and spontaneous, and that it had been prompted by *something*, some past and probably dark experience. He felt another spurt of intense curiosity, all the more destabilising because it was unaccustomed, and he had to resist the urge to barge in and whittle an explanation out of her. Women had always been an open book for him. To suddenly find himself stumped by one whose pages appeared to be firmly glued together was more than a novelty. He was discovering, to his amazement, the power of a challenge.

'Perhaps I should be,' he agreed. 'Maybe I'm more naïve than I think.'

The thought of the man sitting opposite her *ever* being naïve was almost enough to make her burst out laughing.

'Look,' he said quickly, 'I'll lay all my cards on the table. I have a gut feeling that you and I could work well together. I've suffered everything over the past few months, from misfiling to complete incomprehension when it comes to transcribing the gist of some of my more technical letters...' Something of an exaggeration, he thought to himself, but what the heck? 'Not to mention girls who can hardly think straight when they're around me...' He watched her surreptitiously to see what the impact of that comment would be, whether he might read some tacit agreement in her expression, and huffily saw that if anything her eyebrows had flickered upwards in contempt and incredulity.

'I don't think I could bear working for a man who considered himself God's gift to the female sex,' Vicky informed him coldly.

'I don't believe that's *quite* what I—'

'Someone who assumes that every woman in the room is eager and panting to climb into bed with him, someone who can't exist without a comb in his jacket pocket and a sporty car to prop up his self-image—'

'You seem to have totally misunders—'

'Swanning around, giving orders in between gazing at himself in the nearest mirror and then when all's said and done assuming that it's his right to do as he likes with whomever he wants, because he happened to be born with a passably good-looking face—'

'Hold on!'

Just at that very instant the telephone rang, and Vicky leapt up out of her chair and hurried into the hall to answer it. She was still trembling from her tirade because his passing remark had brought back a flood of memories, memories of Shaun and his serial infidelity, his addiction to proving his power over women, his swaggering, arrogant assumption that it was his right to break any female's heart if he so wanted. Her brain was still whirring around in angry circles when she heard Pat Down's voice down the line and it took her a few seconds to register that Chloe would be dropped back earlier than planned.

'I'm ever so sorry, Vicky, but my mum's been rushed to hospital with a heart attack so I shall drop her off in about ten minutes, if that's all right with you.' The voice down the line was just managing to bear up.

'Ten minutes...' Vicky repeated on a sharply indrawn breath.

'Sorry.'

'No, no, that's absolutely fine. Do you need me to hang on to Jess for you?' But no, she would take Jess with her to see her mother and she'd be by in a little under ten minutes.

Vicky hung up and flew into the sitting room like a whirlwind.

'It's time for you to go!' she ordered him frantically. 'I…I…I've suddenly remembered a very important appointment. In fact, that was the person in charge…calling to see whether I was still interested…in the job…'

'On a Saturday?' Max asked, not moving.

With a groan of desperation, Vicky grabbed his arm and began pulling him to his feet. Bad move. It appeared to make him even less inclined to vacate the sofa.

'Get up!' she finally shouted. 'Can't you see I'm in a rush?'

'And I'm trying to figure out why. No respectable company drags interviewees in on a weekend. Have you applied for something shady, perhaps? Some seedy stripping job in a nightclub somewhere?'

'Do I *look* like the sort of girl who's willing to strip in a nightclub?' she virtually screeched, hustling him to the sitting room door and attempting to shoo him out in the style of a chicken trying to get rid of a wolf from its parlour.

'Give me a minute to think about that one,' he said slowly, stopping in his tracks to her intense frustration. She glared at him and he grinned back at her.

It was the first time he had really smiled and the effect was breathtaking. Literally, it made her gasp. It changed the hard contours of his face and gave him a boyish, sexy look that was as far removed from the plastic smiles of his brother as chalk was from cheese.

'Not funny,' she said sharply.

'Take the job?'

In under five minutes there would be the sound of a car stopping outside the house, the ring of the doorbell and her daughter would come bouncing through the front door, bringing her infectious smile, her rosy cheeks and a seething nest of potential catastrophes.

She had to get rid of him.

'All right! *Now* will you please leave my house so that I can get on with…with…with my life?'

He straightened up and looked at her with a shadow of surprise. 'Starting Monday?'

'Starting Monday,' she agreed, hopping in frustration from one leg to another.

She managed to propel him to the front door, which she swiftly pulled open, breathing a sigh of relief that a small blue car wasn't hurtling down the lane in the direction of her cottage.

'Report to Personnel,' he told her, 'then come to my office and we'll take it from there.'

'Goodbye!'

'And perhaps you could do something about your eccentric line in conversation?'

'I shall see you on Monday!' She urged him out of the door and watched as he headed down the short path to the road, making sure that his car was safely out of sight before she closed it back. When it was, she slammed shut the door and leaned heavily against it, wondering what the hell she had just done.

It had been *imperative* that he left the premises before Chloe returned, she argued silently to herself, and what better method of shifting him than to agree to his proposals? Even though the logical, rational side of her brain freely accepted this as a worthwhile argument, the rest of her was appalled at the hole she had dug and into which she had recklessly jumped.

She told herself that she would turn up on Monday and work for a few weeks, then apologetically make her excuses and leave. She mentally listed some of the plus points that could be gained from her manoeuvre. This required more thought, but in the end she decided that, aside from the financial windfall to be had, she would also be able to keep an eye on him and allay his suspicious interest in her which she had sensed from the very beginning. Wasn't it a good idea for her to be in place so that she could make sure that he didn't start telephoning Australia and asking his friend about her? For starters he would learn about the pregnancy. Her connection with his brother might take longer, because she had been adamant about keeping her work life distinct from her private life and had discouraged Shaun from ever showing up at her workplace once they had started dating. But he could find out if he persevered. At least she would be on the spot to laughingly fend off any questions and deter him from snooping. She'd seen the curiosity her odd behaviour had aroused in him and she suspected that he was the sort of man to whom any intrigue was simply something to be unravelled. He could probably do *The Times* crossword in a matter of seconds.

Less palatable was the unpleasant suspicion that something about him had got under her skin. She'd learned so many lessons from Shaun, enough to put her off men for a lifetime. She would rather shoot herself than admit any kind of attraction to his brother.

In the end, though, she now had a problematic situation which she would have to deal with in whatever manner was at her disposal.

CHAPTER THREE

VICKY spent the remainder of the weekend repenting for her reckless agreement to work for Max Forbes. The reason *why* she had rushed into her hasty decision was rapidly forgotten under the onslaught of serious drawbacks. By the time Monday morning rolled around, she found herself slipping on her customary secretarial garb with a leaden heart which was only partially alleviated when, once at the office, she was informed by the personnel officer that Max only worked part-time at this particular office. When the young girl mentioned his name, her eyelids fluttered and her cheeks turned bright red. Vicky wondered sceptically whether *all* the female employees of the company responded in the same way to the mere mention of their boss. If that was the case, then she would have more to contend with than the dangerous fragility of her situation—namely overriding nausea at being surrounded by mesmerised females from nine in the morning to five-thirty at night.

No wonder he rated himself as such a potent sex symbol. She almost clicked her tongue in annoyance.

'I don't suppose he's in London *now*, is he?' she asked the personnel officer, whose name was Mandy and whose fashion statement included disconcertingly long and brightly painted blue fingernails.

'Actually, I believe he's set aside his morning to show you the ropes.'

'Oh, grand!' Vicky exclaimed with dismay, which she hid under a scarily bright smile. The smile remained plastered to her face as she was shown the now familiar route up to his office, only slipping when Mandy deserted her and she found herself pushing back the door to his sanctuary.

After a break of a day and a half, during which the image of him had not left her head for longer than five minutes at a stretch, the sight of him now, in the flesh, was even more alarming than she remembered.

Had he been so *big and muscular* when she had seen him on Saturday or had he somehow grown in the interim? Even sitting behind the desk, reclining in his leather chair, his size seemed to spring out at her and reduce her to nervous, powerless pulp. He had discarded his jacket; his blue and white pin-striped shirt was cuffed to the elbows.

'Ah,' was his first word, which smacked of satisfaction, 'I wasn't too sure that you'd make it here. Good trip in? I gather you've already been through the nitty-gritty with Mandy. I've set aside a couple of hours to fill you in on some of the more straightforward bits of the job, then I'm afraid I've got to leave you to get on with it. So sit down and I'll begin briefing you on your duties.' He paused to recline comfortably in his chair. 'First of all, the coffee machine—it's in the corner of your office outside...'

Vicky, who had primly fished out a notepad and pen from her voluminous handbag, fixed him with a long, beady stare and he grinned at her.

'Just a joke.'

'I do realise that tea- and coffee-making *is* included in my job specification, but I hope it only plays a minor role.' She heard herself with a small, inner groan of disgust. The more addled he made her feel, the more unnatural her patterns of speech seemed to become, and right now she was feeling very, very addled.

'Very minor,' he agreed gravely. 'In fact, I *do* frequently make myself a cup of coffee and it's been known for me to make one for my secretary as well.' He rested his elbows on his desk and brought the tips of his fingers together so that he could survey her over them. It made her feel like a specimen in a laboratory.

'Have you maintained an office in London?' she asked politely. 'I ask because Mandy in Personnel mentioned that you split your time between here and London.'

'And New York, Madrid and Glasgow...I don't suppose you've had a chance to read any of the company literature...' He got up and strode towards a glass-fronted sleekly black bookcase that adorned one wall of the office and extracted a handful of glossy brochures, which he proceeded to hand over to her; then, instead of returning to his swivel chair, he perched on his desk, so that she had an uncomfortably close-up view of his muscular thighs, stretching taut against the fine wool fabric of his trousers.

'No, I haven't.' She idly flicked through one and her hand stopped as she saw a picture of Shaun standing next to Max and between them a man who could only have been their father. The blood in her veins started to curdle.

'My brother,' Max said shortly, following her gaze.

'The three of you founded the business?' Her voice was devoid of expression, even though she discovered that she was surprisingly curious about what his version of past events would be, because there always were the two sides to every story, but a shutter had dropped over his eyes.

'Not quite. You can look at that stuff later, perhaps take it home with you. For now, I'll fill you in on some of the projects we're working on.' He nodded at the door, inviting her to precede him out of his office and into hers which lay just through the door and which housed the filing cabinets. Like all the rest of the furniture in both the offices, the cabinets were all in black wood with chrome handles.

'Normally, my last secretary would have been responsible for taking you through this, but in this case, there's been no *last* secretary and the *last* temp didn't seem to grasp the meaning of the words "filing system", so she would have been of no use whatsoever. Anyway—' he gesticulated towards three cabinets '—the files are kept in there and should be in alphabetical order, although I'd advise you to go through the lot of them yourself. Louise found the alphabet a little exhausting. Those files over there are in the process of being looked at for whatever reason and those need updating. Your computer is over there and I'm afraid there's a stack of work for you to get your teeth into.'

'What kind of work?' Vicky idly went to the large U-shaped desk and flicked through the top file, which seemed comprised of lengthy technical documents and detailed price quotations.

'You'll naturally also be expected to handle all my business engagements and update my diary at least twice a day. Oh, yes, and meetings—I'll expect you to come along to some of the more important ones to take notes. Occasionally, there may be a social function I'll want you to attend.'

'That won't be possible,' Vicky said quickly, without thinking.

'All things in life are possible,' he told her softly, moving across to her. 'How else can anyone ever achieve anything in life, if they automatically assume that some things are not possible? *Why* will the occasional social function be out of the question? Is there any particular reason?'

'No. I just thought…that…social functions might require a more glamorous escort than your secretary…'

'Mmm. I see.' He left it there, neither pressing the point nor, she noticed, denying her claim to plainness. 'Now, files.' He moved smoothly round the desk so that he was facing the computer, switched it on and then beckoned her across to join him.

Standing next to him was an exercise in nerve-tingling embarrassment. He dwarfed her. Shaun had somehow never seemed *that* tall. Maybe he'd just been a little shorter, just as he'd been a little thinner, his features a little more blurred. Perhaps the mould, having been used once, had not quite managed to replicate itself the second time around.

'Familiar with this program?'

Vicky nodded.

'Good, then you'll have no problem finding your way around. You'll have to go through those files and update the computer, and there are one or two problems on a couple of them—discrepancies with the fees, order problems. I'm afraid you're being thrown in at the deep end but you'll have to find your way around the best you can, because the position requires a fair amount of initiative and responsibility. Tell me about your job with James?'

He strolled over to the coffee machine, and while he waited for it to kick into action he turned to face her with his arms folded.

Vicky groped her way for an adequate and truthful account of what she had done as far as work went without implying socialising of any nature. In fact, she had socialised a fair amount with James and his wife Carol, and had even babysat for them on a few occasions. 'I started off as his secretary, but I'm a pretty quick learner and, quite soon, I was being given a fair amount of responsibility. Looking after some of the smaller, more problematic customers, liaising with the service people as well as doing the usual administrative and typing stuff.'

'So you should have no problem coming to grips with all this…' He nodded vaguely at the files. 'I knew it. I took one look at you and knew that you'd be able to do the job with your eyes closed.'

'I haven't even started, as yet,' Vicky informed him warily. Heaping praise on her before she even got going was not so good, considering her long-range plan to quit the job as soon as was possible, without arousing needless suspicion.

'I think the first thing we need to sort out is my diary for the next month...' He went into his office and returned several seconds later with an electronic diary and a conventional leatherbound one, which he handed to her. 'Right. Now, let's start with tomorrow...' He pulled across one of the spare chairs from in front of the desk and strategically positioned it next to her so that, while he was no longer towering over her, he was now so close to her that with the flick of his pen on the keypad, his forearm casually but insistently brushed hers. She kept flicking sidelong, uncomfortable glances at the fine dark hairs sprinkling his powerful arms. He seemed so much more *real* than his twin, so much more *substantial*.

He began listing, very rapidly, his plans for the day, which she checked against the entries in the black diary. Some of the handwriting was poor enough to require several long seconds of tortuous interpretation and, after one particularly puzzling entry, she glanced up to find him looking at her.

'I'm beginning to understand what you meant by problems with temps,' she said with the ghost of a smile. 'If the filing system bears any resemblance to the handwriting in here, then I shall have several hours sorting out some basic stuff before I can even start to do my job.'

'Didn't I tell you?' Up close, as he was, he noticed that her skin was as flawlessly smooth as it appeared to be from a distance, and her hair, severely tied back, still managed to break free around her ears so that the tiny tendrils gave her the look of a saint whose halo had slipped to one side. Feeling his arm brush against hers, a passing touch that he could have avoided but chose not to, filled him with an almost sinful sense of excitement. He'd never known how powerful female modesty could be. Here she was, dressed in three times as much clothing as the woman he had last dated—Lord, three months ago—and yet the effect of all those clothes on him was positively suffocating. She had removed her jacket, but her blouse was buttoned up prudishly to the neck with small pearl buttons of the type worn by grannies. He could indistinctly make out the outline of her bra underneath. He wondered, and this sent a little electric shock to his groin, what it would feel like to undo those prim buttons, fingers touching skin underneath the shirt, anticipation building to a frenzy. He imagined her hands loosely tied to the bedstead with silk scarves while he undressed her, taking his time and exploring each exposed bit of skin with his tongue. He would drive her wild, enjoying her uncontrolled writhing. Naturally she would plead with him not to stop, to rip aside her bra and relieve her aching breasts with his mouth.

When he glanced her way, it was to find her looking at him as though she could read every salaciously impure thought in his head, and he flushed darkly. Good heavens! The woman was his *secretary*!

'Believe me now?' he asked roughly, sounding, he thought, the Big Bad Wolf when confronted with Little Red Riding Hood. He grinned to himself at the unconscious parallel, because right now he would have liked nothing better than to eat her up, every inch of her defensive little body, starting with her pale, slender neck and moving all the way down to the patch of hair between her thighs that would naturally be daintily shielded behind granny-style underwear.

He cleared his throat and dragged his thoughts back to meetings, calendars and business appointments. She was asking him something and he made a huge effort to concentrate and reply in a normal voice.

'I see you're in London twice this week,' she was saying, gazing down with satisfaction at the diary entries. Two business meetings in Temple, another in Uxbridge.

'So I am. Perhaps—' he frowned '—I ought to cancel those and spend a bit more time here, until you get accustomed to the running of the office.'

Vicky was quick to sit on any such suggestion. 'There's no need for that.' She realised that his recumbent arm was too close for comfort, and she discreetly but firmly edged hers away. 'In fact, having a couple of days on my own will be perfect for me to fill myself in on the files and the customers and also catch up with some of that backlog of typing.'

He could see her trying very hard to look regretful and felt a sulky and childish tug on his masculine pride that the thought of spending time along with him in the office was obviously a fate only slightly better than death, as far as she was concerned. What appealing work experience lay in store for both of them at this rate!

'Well, you can't miraculously work your way through *everything* on your own. I'm going to have to answer a few questions, presumably.' Now, he sounded piqued. The cool, self-confident, self-assured, mature and winningly charming adult seemed to have been replaced by a sulking thirteen-year-old. Where that emotion had come from he had no idea as it had never been in evidence before.

'I realise that,' Vicky said, briefly looking at him and then resuming her perusal of the file in front of her.

'Whenever I need you to help, I shall ask. I think finding my way around the business and *what you do here* is going to take the longest. I'll read up all the company literature, but Mrs Hogg—'

'Ms Hogg.'

'I beg your pardon?'

'*Ms* Hogg. Geraldine prefers good, healthy outdoor pursuits with her formidable sister to the company of men any day of the week.' He grinned and she reluctantly grinned back.

'Well, as I was saying...' What *had* she been saying? '*Ms* Hogg didn't get much of a chance to fill me in on this particular branch of your company. She mentioned that it's a fairly new concern—'

'But growing at an almost unprecedented rate,' he carried on for her, 'hence my involvement. Virtually all of our customers are new to us and have to be treated with kid gloves, aside from one or two whose mother company is based in London and whose subsidiaries coincidentally operate in this general area. I'm pretty busy for the rest of the day, but I can always pop over to your house some time after wor—'

'No!' Vicky heard the panic in her voice with alarm. The important thing was to lull any suspicions he might have of her to sleep, not stoke them into a frenzy by over-reacting to obvious situations. 'I mean, I have very...very definite views on business and pleasure.'

'Does that mean that you shed your working personality the minute you walk out of the office building?' He stared at her narrowly, head cocked insolently to one side, as though conjuring up a mental picture. 'Intriguing. As the office doors swing shut behind you, do you wrench the clips out of your hair and hitch up your neat, little tailored skirt?'

'Of course I don't,' Vicky said coolly. 'I just think that it's important to separate leisure time from work time, or else the two begin flowing into one another and somewhere down the road you realise that there's no part of your life that isn't free from work.' *Neat, little tailored skirt?* How could four small words be invested with such a derogatory meaning? He made her sound like an old age pensioner and, without thinking, she let her fingers flutter to the top button of her shirt, firmly done up, protecting her from unwanted attention. She had never been like this. There had been a time, not *that* long ago, when she'd used to wear short skirts and pretty, attractive tops, but that had been before she had learnt that prudery was the only defence against Shaun's lecherous hands. The sight of her primly buttoned up had sometimes been enough to deter him from invading her body and she had grown accustomed to the way of dressing until now, she realised with a start, most of her clothes conformed to the prissy, unadventurous image she had meticulously cultivated over time.

'But is it such a good idea to compartmentalise your life? Don't you find that a little unhealthy?' He'd pushed his chair a little way away from hers to enable him to scrutinise her face, which was now going a deep shade of pink. It occurred to her that they had successfully managed to veer away from the point of their conversation, which was namely to brief her on office business, and she struggled to find a way of bringing it back to the matter in hand. While she was busy grappling with the problem, he filled the brief silence with his sudden interest in her private life.

'Reminds me of a split personality,' he said thoughtfully, and she felt her hackles rise at the insinuation.

'I assure you I'm *perfectly normal*,' Vicky informed him

in a voice that suggested closure of the topic. She meaningfully peered at the file in front of her, even fetching out a piece of paper to stare at it with frowning concentration, though her eyes weren't registering much of what was written there.

'I never implied that you weren't!' he protested in an offended voice. 'I just think that it's perfectly natural for work to spill over sometimes into leisure.'

'Well, perhaps you're right,' Vicky said with a shrug. 'Are you contactable when you're in London or would you rather problems waited until you returned here?'

'You can e-mail me any time, or telephone, of course, although I'm not often in the office.' He allowed an acceptable period of silence to stretch between them, then he said in a considering tone, 'Do you know, it's been my experience that women who are fanatically guarded about their private life usually have something to hide...?'

He had unknowingly hit jackpot. He could sense it in the stillness of her body, which only lasted a matter of seconds but was enough to tell an entire story of its own.

'I have nothing to hide,' she informed him icily, 'and at the risk of sounding impertinent on my first day here, I should just like to say that I resent your prying into my private life...'

'I didn't realise that I was *prying* into your private life, I *thought* that I was making a general statement...' Her tone of voice didn't appear to have put him off his stride and she saw, with dismay, the gleam lurking seductively in his eyes. 'Of course—' he dropped his eyes and inspected his nails briefly '—you're entitled to your privacy, and if you have something that you're ashamed of...'

'I am *not* ashamed of *anything*!'

'Okay! Okay!' It was the oldest trick in the book and she knew it. He was making a show of backing away from confrontation while simultaneously appearing doubtful of her protestations of innocence.

'What could I have to be ashamed of?' she couldn't help demanding indignantly, and this was met by a theatrical shrug of his broad shoulders.

'Nothing.'

Vicky made the inarticulate sound of someone whose feathers have been severely ruffled.

'Unless,' he said as an afterthought, 'it's something to do with a man.' He flicked a quick look at her to see how this one registered but her normal serenity was well and truly back in place. 'You know, you're entitled to have whatever relationships you want, be they with married men…'

Vicky, recognising that he was fishing for information, maintained her studious silence, chewing her lip as she peered down at sheaths of paper in a business like manner.

This was what she had feared most, this willingness on his part to cheerfully overstep the mark. He had no respect for anyone's limits. If he got it into his head that jumping over them was what he wanted to do, then jump over them he would, and with a grin on his face.

'Or even married women…' He didn't seriously believe that that was a possibility but he decided to voice his thoughts anyway, if only to keep this enticing conversation on the go. As expected, she shot him a dry look and didn't bother to say anything.

'Or perhaps it's a toy boy? These things *do* happen…'

'I'm not old enough for a toy boy,' Vicky pointed out with a sigh of resignation. 'No married men, *or women, for that matter*, no toy boy, no geriatric in his seventies, no *skeletons*, in fact…' She sounded pleasingly truthful and couldn't resist a smug smile in his direction.

'Everyone has a skeleton or two,' he said quickly, and she raised her eyebrows at him.

He wasn't going to get anywhere with this one. She was now looking at him with crisp efficiency, raring to get going with whatever folder she'd been fingering for the past fifteen minutes. He admitted defeat, and for the next two hours they worked alongside one another. Instead of wasting time going through files individually, he dictated letters, briefly giving her a lowdown on each account as he covered them.

She picked things up fast. He'd spent so many months battling with various levels of incompetence that it was sheer bliss to work with someone who was capable of following his pace. Her questions were clipped and relevant, she grasped what she needed to do without requiring a lengthy process of repetition, and by the time Maria on Switchboard began putting through his calls once again he felt confident enough to leave her on her own to get on with things.

Through the office partition, he could see a sliver of her at her desk, one hand holding a pen, which she lightly tapped as she inspected whatever she had just typed onto the computer. She had shoved her hair into a bun, and ever so often she would absent-mindedly reposition her rebellious curls.

Max rolled his chair a few vital inches to the left, without altering the tenor of his conversation on the telephone, and guiltily watched her as she worked. It made him feel a bit like a lecher so, after a few minutes, he rolled himself back in front of his desk and made an effort to swivel towards the window behind him so that he no longer felt like a voyeur.

He only realised how keyed-up he was to her presence

when she politely peeped into his office forty minutes later with a question.

'I've been going through the filing cabinets,' she began, and he indicated the chair for her to sit.

'And...?'

'It appears that two files have been made of this account, and filed under separate names.' Vicky handed him the files, which boasted two different sets of handwriting. 'Problem is that the information in both doesn't correspond, even though it's all to do with the same thing. It looks as though one of your secretaries dealt with something three months ago and then misfiled the folder. When the problem recurred, her replacement started a new file and basically told the client the complete opposite of what had been said to him previously.' She stood up and leaned forward, flicking open both the files and then carefully indicating what she meant. One long strand of wayward hair escaped and skirted her neck, coiling in a perfect red-gold corkscrew curl.

'Leave it with me. I'll deal with it.'

'I don't mind...' She glanced and met his eyes, then quickly lowered hers. 'Sorry. Overstepping my brief. I suppose I was so accustomed to dealing with these types of customer problems at my last job in Australia that I could find it easy to slip back into my old ways.' She reminded herself that that would be impossible, since her time allotment for this particular job was a matter of weeks rather than years. Any slipping she would be doing would be out of the office door and into the nearest employment agency.

'I have an idea,' he said slowly, pushing himself back from his desk and tilting a bit on the chair. 'Why don't we pay a few visits to some of the more critical clients? If you meet them, then you can put a face to the voice at the end of the telephone and so can they. Have a look at my diary and fill me in on what I'm up to on...let's see...next Tuesday. We can spend a couple of hours with each and have a break for lunch at one of the better country pubs around here.'

Vicky began calculating in her head whether Brenda, her childminder, would be able to cover for her next Tuesday. Chloe would have to miss her after-school swimming lesson, but that was fine. She hated them anyway. If they managed to clear everything up no later than six in the evening, then there should be no problem at all.

She looked at him to find him staring at her with hooded interest.

'I'll get your diary,' she said hurriedly, fleeing the office before he could begin quizzing her on further evidence of her mysterious secret life. As she fished for the diary from the drawer of her desk, she wondered whether she shouldn't just head him off by fabricating something that might satisfy his masculine curiosity. It would have to be something worth secreting away, yet nowhere near the truth. Perhaps, she thought, she could invent a double life as a stripper. That would shut him up, she was sure.

As she headed back into the office, her mouth was curved into a small smile at her ludicrous but amusing secret plan.

'Share the joke?'

She raised her eyes to his but she didn't see him. What she saw, in fact, was a stage in a darkened room on which she wove with sensuous, semi-naked abandon, watched hungrily by the man sitting opposite her at the desk. Her mind was filled suddenly and sickening with an erotic image that was strong enough to blow her off her feet. She very quickly sat down, just in case, and delved blindly into the black diary on her lap, furiously flicking through the pages until her trembling fingers lighted onto the correct one.

She mumbled something about there being no joke to share, making sure that she kept her eyes firmly averted from his face, and then said crisply, 'Tuesday looks fine. If you tell me what clients you'd like to visit, then I can try and arrange them.' She was still speaking to the diary. In a minute, when her head had completely cleared of its treacherous suggestion, she would resume normal behaviour patterns.

'If we meet the first, Prior and Truman, at nine, then we can probably fit Robins in before lunch. Make sure that you leave a two-hour window for lunch, say between one and three, then a couple more and we can call it a day.'

'And which client would you like to take to lunch?' Her heart rate was getting back to its normal speed, thankfully, and she risked a look at him.

'None. I think you and I could benefit from a bit of uninterrupted time together.' He let the words sink in, then added, 'To go through any little work problems you might have encountered that you need to ask me about.' He wasn't *smiling*, she noticed, when he said this, but there was the *feeling* of a smile tugging at his mouth and she shot him a quenchingly professional look, just in case there was anything there that needed snuffing out.

Shaun had made her wise to the manipulations of the flirt. He himself had used more obvious tactics. He had often spread himself across her desk, before she'd insisted that he no longer come into her workplace, making sure that she'd had nowhere else to look but at some part of his reclining body; then, later, the big gestures of extravagant flowers and expensive dinners in the places where to be seen was to step up two notches on your street cred rating. The showy manoeuvres had lasted the length of time it had taken to get her into bed, then gradually they had dwindled, until the day had arrived when the flowers and expensive dinners became things of the past. She would always, at the back of her mind, equate pregnancy with misery, because it was then that the seriously destructive verbal abuse had really begun, the taunts that would reduce her to uncontrollable weeping, the slamming of doors and jeering that had made her want to disappear from the face of the earth.

She wondered whether Max Forbes was cut from the same cloth, just a different pattern. The more she saw of him, the more confused she was becoming, because her instincts were telling her that he was nothing like his brother, even though she was disillusioned enough to know that instincts had a nasty way of being wrong.

Then, when her irritating speculations had reached a peak, she told herself that none of it mattered a jot anyway because, whether he was like his brother or in fact a saint in the making, he was still a dangerous and unwanted intruder in her life.

'Right. Anything else?' he asked, pushing his chair back and stretching. He walked across to the door, on the back of which hung his jacket, slung negligently over the hook despite the hanger that was sitting there gathering dust. 'I've got a couple of important meetings and, as you know, I'll be out of the office tomorrow. Think you can cope?'

'I'll do my best,' Vicky told him. She could feel an unwelcome stir of excitement at the prospect of all the work that lay ahead of her. If Max Forbes thought that months of unsatisfactory temps was frustrating, then she could deliver a sermon of her own on the dissatisfaction of one very proficient temp, namely herself, who had spent the past few months photocopying, photocopying and doing yet more photocopying. In between she had managed to run errands that no one else wanted to run, do filing that had been studiously avoided for decades and transferred enough tedious information from sheets of paper to computer to make her goggle-eyed.

'You know where you can reach me. All my numbers, including the one for my flat in Fulham, are at the front of your diary.'

'I shouldn't think that anything *that* urgent will come up that requires me to get in touch with you at your home.'

'You can never tell,' he said, slinging on his jacket and patting the pocket to make sure that his cellular phone was present and correct.

Vicky, who had automatically followed him to the door, now said with wry amusement, 'You're a company director, not a highly pressurised neurosurgeon on call. Don't you think that life *might* go on if you aren't around for a couple of days?' Then she suddenly remembered that she was supposed to be working for him. When she wasn't on guard, it was all too easy to relax with him. Considering that one of the few advantages to taking this job, so she'd repeatedly told herself, was the fact that she would be keyed up and mentally alert to spot and ward off any potential danger, allowing herself to relax was not on the agenda.

'Maybe,' he admitted reluctantly, favouring her with one of those slow, specialty smiles which he seemed to do unconsciously. He opened the door and turned to look down at her. 'Maybe not. But don't worry, anyway. I'll be back soon enough.'

The words sounded like an ominous warning in the sunlit office and attached themselves to the growing line of worries complicating her life.

Or so it suddenly seemed.

CHAPTER FOUR

NEXT TUESDAY, which had seemed a million years away, arrived with stupendous speed.

During his two days out of the office, Vicky had jumped into the deep waters of bad filing, customer queries, letters to be typed, memos and phone calls and e-mails and faxes and things to sort out so that they were understandable to *her*. The time had whisked by. Every so often she would dutifully tell herself that she wouldn't be around long enough to see the benefits of some of the systems she was putting in place, but already a little voice at the back of her mind was beginning to sing a different tune.

Well, why would he find out about Chloe? He hadn't so far, and he had stopped asking difficult questions. Perhaps his nosy curiosity had all been part of his interviewing methods, to make sure that she could handle his temperament. Of course, she wouldn't stay there forever, but why not for a bit longer than she had planned? Why not? The money was brilliant, better than anything she could ever hope to earn in a million years around Warwick. Or around London, for that matter. She would be able to put a bit aside, and wouldn't that come in handy for all the building work that needed doing on her house? The place seemed to be falling down around her ears and she had to find the money to do repair work from somewhere. Hadn't she? And the work was going to be exciting. She was so sick of being given the dross as a temp; why not enjoy the sudden opportunity to have a few responsibilities? Yes, of course it was dangerous being around the

*man, even though he knew nothing of her personal life.
But it was a danger she could handle. The fact that she
was aware of it would be enough to deaden its force. She
would keep him at a distance. In effect, she would use him,
use him for the fabulous pay cheque at the end of the
month and the fantastic chance to satisfy her need for an
invigorating career, and if he started asking questions
again or prying into her personal life, then she would
dump the job immediately. And what was wrong with that?
Hadn't she been well and truly used by that brother of
his? In fact, she could look on it as a kind of game, with
her in possession of all the rules. She knew, after all, all
about him, but he knew nothing about her. So who was
going to have the last laugh? All she needed was to be
careful and she could enjoy the situation instead of being
petrified.*

By the following Monday, she'd made significant in-
roads into some of the backlog that had stockpiled on her
desk, including various dusty letters which had been forgotten or ignored during the rapid succession of unsuc-
cessful temps.

Max was out of the office more than he was in it, and
when he *was* in, he spent most of his time locked in his
office, on the phone or on the fax or in front of his computer, frowning at rows upon rows of numbers.

Now, as she cleared her desk in anticipation of going
home, she stole a quick look at him through the smoked
glass partition. Seen like this, he was less intimidating than
he was in the flesh. He was reduced to a darkish shape
which she could easily handle.

Not, she thought smugly, whisking her pens and pencils
into the drawer and clicking it shut, that he was proving
to be a problem at all. In fact, there were times when she
very nearly forgot the dark connection that ran between

them like an unseen, pulsating vein. She still couldn't quite manage to slot him into the harmless category that she would have liked, he was just too overwhelming for that, but at least she no longer looked at him with the terror of a rabbit caught in headlights.

And Chloe was happier and more relaxed than she had been since they returned to England.

Vicky pondered this for a minute. The only explanation she could find was that her daughter had somehow picked up her inexplicable contentment at work with her efficient, childish antennae and was happier for it.

She knocked briefly on Max's interconnecting door, while slinging on her jacket and poked her head around it to tell him that she was off.

He crooked his finger at her, beckoning her to enter, and Vicky quickly glanced at her watch, estimating how much time she could spare for a quick chat. She was accustomed to picking up Chloe from the childminder at a little after five-thirty, which didn't give her very long in terms of travel. She could, she knew, leave her there longer, but she hated doing that. It was enough of a wrench not being able to collect her directly from school at three-thirty, without prolonging her absence. And she didn't want to start taking advantage of Brenda's good nature.

'*If* you can spare the time,' he said drily, tilting back in the chair with his hands clasped behind his head.

Vicky went in, but remained standing and didn't shut the door behind her. The point was not lost on her boss, who looked at her with wry amusement.

'How are you enjoying the job so far?'

'It's early days yet.' No point committing herself to an enthusiastic response just yet. For starters, if she decided to leave in the very near future, she wanted to be able to hang on to the tried and tested excuse about it not being

her cup of tea after all. And, additionally, she didn't want
to give him the opportunity to imagine that he had been
right all along.

'You seem to have picked it up very well, from what
I've seen.'

'You've been out of the office most of the time,' Vicky
pointed out.

'I've accessed some of the files you were due to update
on the computer and it's all been done, and unless you've
eaten the outstanding paperwork most of that has been
done as well.' He sat forward and began fiddling with his
fountain pen, a burgundy Mont Blanc with a solid gold
trim. 'And tomorrow we've got your first introduction to
clients. Nervous?'

Vicky, who couldn't reasonably look at her watch without it being obvious, fidgeted from one foot to the other
and tried not to think about the dash she would have to
get to her childminder by five-thirty.

'Looking forward to it.'

'I apologise for not being around a bit more to show
you the ropes, considering it's early days here for you...'
He began tapping the closed fountain pen on the surface
of his desk and she wondered why he had bothered to ask
her into his office and enquire about her levels of happiness if he was that impatient to get going. Was he under
the mistaken impression that she wanted to see him?

'It's no problem.'

'You must have a lot of questions to ask.' His grey eyes
swept over her, taking in her neat uniform of knee-length
skirt, crisp cotton blouse and grey jacket which was now
in place, obliterating all traces of femininity.

The world of fashion had a lot to answer for when it
came to suits for women, he thought. It was difficult to
imagine anything more conducive to killing the male imag-

ination. He decided that his office would be far better served were she to wear something a little less military, perhaps a silky short mini skirt and a clinging wet shirt, worn braless.

He grinned inwardly at the chauvinistic irreverence of his thoughts. He personally knew several extremely high-powered female executives who would hang, draw and quarter him had they any insight into his current line of thinking. They would all be particularly disgusted, since he had always led the way when it came to equality between the sexes. He'd made it a company policy that pay reflected talent rather than gender, and females in positions of power had always been actively condoned within the various branches of his huge, global network of companies.

As far as he was concerned, the work environment was not a cat-walk and inappropriate dressing was discouraged.

Right now, however, he thought that some inappropriate dressing would do just nicely.

'No, none that I can think of offhand.'

'Sorry?' He realised sheepishly that his drifting thoughts had gone further than he thought.

'I *said*—'

'We can discuss them over dinner.'

'I beg your pardon?'

'Your questions. We can discuss them over dinner. Fewer interruptions than if we tried to sort them out here, during the day. I could pick you up around seven-thirty. How does that sound?'

'No, thank you.'

The blunt refusal was like a bucket of cold water thrown gaily over his head. The worst thing was that he shouldn't have asked her out in the first place. He might tell himself that it was business, but he knew that that couldn't have been further from the truth. He looked at her stubborn, shuttered face, her full mouth drawn into a firm, disapproving line, and felt the kick of adolescent disappointment.

Except for the fact that he wasn't an adolescent.

'Why not?' he heard himself ask. 'Don't imagine that this is anything other than work.' With a trace of satisfaction, he saw her translucent skin suffuse with pink colour and some vague notion of reestablishing his bruised male pride made him pursue the point with more tenacity than was warranted. 'Your virtue is absolutely secure with me, my dear.' Pale pink was becoming a shade darker. He noted that she was no longer looking at him but staring fixedly in the region of her shoes. 'In fact, I've always believed it vitally important that sex and work don't mix. The combination is usually lethal. I simply thought that you might feel a bit more relaxed away from the office, might find it easier to concentrate on any problems you might have without the constant interruption of telephones and people popping in and out. Naturally, if you have other, more pressing engagements…'

He glanced idly down at a sheaf of paper on the desk, letting her know, without putting it in so many words, that her reply was fairly unimportant but that he was, at the end of the day, *her boss*.

'Yes, I have actually,' Vicky told him. 'In fact, I really must be on my way…' There was a trace of guilty apology in her voice that made him clench his teeth together in frustration.

'I don't approve of clock-watching,' he said grimly. Now his jaw was beginning to ache and he slowly relaxed his muscles. He could tell that she was frazzled by his attitude but really, *what*, at this hour of the afternoon, could *possibly* be so important? He could understand that she might have plans later on in the evening, but at *five-fifteen in the afternoon*? And those plans obviously weren't innocent. If she had to scurry off to the dentist or the hairdresser or to the corner shop before it closed, then she would have said so.

He felt that spark of intense curiosity and allied with it was something more disturbing. Jealousy. *Jealousy*! It seemed that the woman was stirring up a viper's nest of unprecedented emotions. He stared at her with brooding resentment and thought that the only thing that could bring a guilty flush like that to a woman's cheeks was a man. Illicit afternoon sex. All that baloney about no skeletons in the cupboard and having nothing to hide had been pure fabrication. Did she imagine that he would care one way or another whether she was having an affair with a married man? Did she think that he was moralistic enough to sack her because she might be behaving inappropriately? Didn't the woman know that this was no longer the Victorian era?

Illicit afternoon sex. Illicit sex in the afternoon. Illicit, frantic, steamy sex in the afternoon, with the curtains drawn. Or maybe with the curtains *undrawn*. Who knew? A quiet knock on the door and she would let him in. A small, insignificant office worker with no personality to speak of and a drastically receding hairline, and upstairs they would go, to fling off their clothes and get down to the pressing business of *illicit afternoon sex*.

His mind played with the evolving scenario until he was forced to break the lengthening silence.

'Perhaps I should give you a few days' notice if I intend to keep you five minutes after you're due to leave.' His voice was laced with cold sarcasm and he unobtrusively tried to massage his jawline with his hand.

'Oh, five minutes is no problem,' Vicky said awkwardly. 'I just…you know, I'm very busy with the house…there's

always someone due to come round…plumbers…
electricians…you know…' Her voice trailed away into
awkward silence and he nodded briefly at her.

'I'll see you tomorrow. You'll have to be here by eight-
thirty if we're to get to Prior and Truman by nine.'

Vicky nodded, relieved that she had received her signal
to depart. She drove like a maniac back to her childminder's house, but even when she and Chloe were back
home, doing all the usual stuff they did in the evening, she
carried on feeling a little jumpy. As though any minute,
and without notice, she would look up and see Max
Forbes's dark, mocking face staring at her through the sitting room window. Like an avenging angel, but with nothing of the angel about him. An avenging devil.

Chloe wanted chicken nuggets for her dinner. She had
originally wanted a McDonald's, but had graciously allowed herself to be persuaded into ordinary chicken nuggets at home on the understanding that pudding, in the
form of ice cream and chocolate buttons, would be abun-
dant.

Vicky raced around the kitchen while her daughter sat
at the kitchen table and chatted about school, intermittently
drawing a family portrait that bore no resemblance to their
family, or any family for that matter, at least of the human
variety.

She hadn't bothered to get out of her working clothes
and she felt disgruntled and sticky. Out of the corner of
her eye she looked at her daughter, who was gravely intent
on her task at hand, her dark hair swinging past her satin-
smooth baby face, and felt a jolt of fear.

What was she doing? Even here, in her own house, she
half felt as though she needed to look over her shoulder,
just in case Max appeared unexpectedly, like a rabbit pop-

ping out of a hat. So what if the money was a godsend, so what if she actually was discovering that the job was as exciting as she'd thought it would be? She was still playing with fire and everyone knew what happened to foolish women who played with fire. They got burnt.

She gazed lovingly at Chloe and realised that the chicken nuggets were getting burnt.

The following morning, she made a decision. She would begin laying the groundwork for her eventual, inevitable and sooner-than-expected resignation.

She couldn't bring herself to work less hard or to do any of her jobs carelessly and thereby ensure dismissal. It just wasn't in her nature. Instead, she decided to go down the road of little hints.

He was in the office and waiting for her when she arrived with fifteen minutes to spare. He had fetched out a stack of files and, in a quarter of an hour, proceeded to fill her in on the people she would be meeting, the way their company operated and what part they played in the Forbes Corporation. In between, she made them both a cup of coffee while he perched indolently on her desk and rattled off information.

It felt comfortable. She dabbled around him, listening and taking in every word, carefully sticking a couple of pens into the briefcase which she had seen fit to buy shortly after starting the job and some paper, in case she wanted to take notes. Every so often she paused, asked a question, then proceeded with what she had been doing.

By a quarter to nine they were ready to leave, and she was fairly confident that she wouldn't find herself too much out of her depth.

What she hadn't been prepared for was how much she would enjoy the experience of being on the move with Max Forbes, meeting clients, playing a subdued but appreciated second fiddle to him. When his attention was focused elsewhere, as it was throughout the day, she could watch him with shameless interest and, with each passing minute, the respect which she'd felt for him from the very beginning became more grounded. She could now barely believe that he and Shaun had been related at all, never mind the intimate connection they had shared. Were it not for the physical resemblance, which was beginning to get a bit blurred in her mind as it was, she would have said that as two people the brothers could not have been further apart.

Lunch at a pub in the middle of the countryside, yet not incredibly far from the nearest town, was a one-hour affair which sped past. They discussed the clients they had seen, the ways in which they interacted with the property development side of the Forbes company. Max talked about New York, which was as personal as he got, and in turn Vicky chatted about living in Warwick as opposed to living on the other side of the world, without giving away too much information.

By the time they had finished with their last client at a little after three, it was pointless returning to the office.

'My car's still there,' Vicky pointed out.

'I'll give you a lift home. You can always take a taxi in to work in the morning.'

'No. That won't do.' She stared remotely out of the window, vaguely looking at the wide open spaces, dotted with the occasional house or barn conversion. They were still a little distance out of the city centre and unfortunately on the wrong side of Warwick as far as the office was concerned.

'Why won't it do?' Max asked with a hint of impatience.

'I like having my car,' Vicky said stubbornly. 'There's no public transport to speak of from my house and I don't like to think about what I'd do if something happened and I needed to get somewhere fast.'

'Something like what?' He seemed to know where he was going, and fortunately it was more or less in the direction of the office, so she was less jumpy than she might have been otherwise at the tenor of his question.

'Oh, I don't know.' She shrugged and lazily slid her eyes across to him, mentally taking in the forcefulness of his profile, the harsh cut of his features, the dark, springy hair that seemed as defiant as hers when it came to being controlled. Even though his, unlike hers, was a less obvious colour. Chloe would have that very same thick, black hair, offset by those amazing grey eyes. She felt another twinge of uneasiness, which she stifled, at least momentarily.

'I could fall over and break something...'

'In that case, you wouldn't be able to drive for help.'

'Or I could burn myself badly with a saucepan of hot milk...'

'Mm. Casualty, but still no car would be needed. You'd have to call for help.'

'Okay. I could discover at eight in the evening that I've run out of instant coffee and I desperately need to go out and buy some more from the corner shop...'

'So now you tell me that you're addicted to coffee.' There was sudden rich humour in his voice and it made her flush with excited pleasure and look quickly away from his curving mouth. 'Mood swings, you know—bouts of sudden depression, quite unpredictable...'

'Who? What?'

'Coffee addicts...' He chuckled and she automatically grinned in response.

'Do you know,' she murmured, 'I've spent years wondering about those strange personality defects of mine?

Thank you so much for sorting it out for me. Coffee addiction. Tomorrow I'm a changed person.'

This time he laughed, a deep-throated, appreciative laugh, and she felt another quick stab of pleasure.

'Okay,' he conceded, 'we'll head back to the office, but why don't we play truant and have a bit of time out rather than go back to work?'

'Play truant? A bit of time out?' She wasn't looking at him but she was smiling, weirdly relaxed and happy, despite all those misgivings which kept popping up with nagging regularity. In a little while, she would erect her defences once more. But, for the minute, sitting alongside him in his powerful car, after an unexpectedly enjoyable day, she felt too lazy to get worked up. 'Surely,' she continued, 'those are not the words of an empire builder? If they are, then I reckon I could go out and build one or two empires myself.' Cold winter sunshine glinted across the countryside, giving everything a hard edge.

'Everyone needs a bit of truancy now and again, especially when in the right company,' he murmured, more to himself than to her, so that she had to strain to hear him, and even then she couldn't be sure that she had heard correctly. 'I have an idea.'

'What?' She turned to look at him.

'I live a matter of minutes away from the office. We could go there, and before you start protesting, I'm merely suggesting it because I've had quite a bit of building work done on my place and, if you decide to stay with the firm, you'd be entitled to reduced costs. You could get an idea of the standard of work the company is capable of.'

'I haven't decided whether I'm staying or not,' Vicky said feebly, uncomfortably aware that she was raising the point because she knew she had to and not because she wanted to.

'What do you mean by that?' he asked sharply, and Vicky felt the cut of his eyes flick over to her.

She squirmed a bit in the seat and cleared her throat. 'Well, I *am* on probation...' she began, sliding away from the argument looming ahead on the horizon. 'You might very well find that I'm not suitable for the job and...and...well, I want to give it a bit of time before I make my mind up as well,' she trailed on evasively.

'Why?' he demanded. 'Are there problems that you haven't told me about? Some aspect of the work proving too difficult?'

'No! I was just speaking...hypothetically.' She cleared her throat again in an attempt to establish control over her unconvincing arguments.

While they had been talking and her attention had been distracted, he'd driven quickly and expertly back to his house and, before she could protest, he was pulling up the drive and killing the engine.

His house was in one of the many rural retreats that nestled alongside the city centre, within twenty minutes' driving distance, yet with a remote feel that came from being surrounded by open land. The front garden was set back from the road and hidden behind a luxuriant hedge that had been trimmed with awe-inspiring precision.

'I...I d-didn't realise you were bringing me to your house,' Vicky stammered, stepping out of the car and glancing at her watch.

'Oh. I thought I mentioned it.' He was unlocking the front door, his back to her, and she frowned at him, wondering why she felt as though she had been skilfully manoeuvred. He pushed open the door and stood aside to let her pass. Hesitantly, she brushed past him, feeling the hairs on her arm stand on end at the slight contact, then she was inside a compact hallway, with rich wooden flooring. The

banister curved upwards to rooms that were left to her
imagination but, as far as she could see, the ones on the
ground floor had been decorated with flair and taste.

'Not my own,' he confessed, following her appreciative
gaze around her. 'Two ladies armed with some of the
weightiest books I have ever seen managed to persuade
me that all of this—' he spread his arm in a sweeping
gesture to encompass the house '—was precisely what I
wanted.'

'And was it?' She stepped a little more confidently into
the hall, and continued to survey the clever subdued oat-
meal colours that lent startling emphasis to the paintings
hanging on the walls and the depth of the maple flooring.
Through some of the half-opened doors, which promised
a house bigger and more complex than it appeared from
the outside, she could see that the pale canvas theme continued throughout, with splashes of deep green or vibrant
terracotta bringing bursts of intermittent colour.

'Well, I like it, so it would appear so.' He laughed under
his breath and she smiled in response.

'I must say, I have absolutely no eye for interior design
either,' she admitted, 'so two ladies with large books
would do quite nicely for me as well.'

'It could be arranged,' he murmured, heading off out of
the hall and expecting her to follow. Which she did.

She found herself in a kitchen which was expensively
furnished with all the latest gadgets in evidence. None of
them looked as though they had been touched. Only the
semi-blackened kettle on the Aga hinted that someone actually used the kitchen, and the kitchen table, she was
pleased to see, seemed to have an air of history about it.

'I take it you don't cook,' she said. 'Everything looks
brand-new.'

'Everything *is* brand-new. The decorators only cleared off about a week ago. Coffee?'

She was so accustomed to making coffee for him at work that the sudden role reversal, and the even more disturbing hint of intimacy in the situation, made her flush.

'Perhaps a quick cup.' Before any silence could develop between them, she began speaking rapidly, almost eating up her words, asking him about the building work that had been done, how long it had taken, whether he was pleased with the house, if there was anything else that required doing. She would have happily rattled on about the condition of her split ends if it had succeeded in masking her awareness of where she was. In Max Forbes's house. Alone. No computer, fax machine or ringing telephone to assert the appropriate differences between them.

To her further unease, he began loosening his tie, tugging at it with one hand while he poured hot water into two mugs with the other. Her eyes clamped onto his long fingers as they pulled at the tie and she had to blink a few times to clear her head. He was saying something about walls that had needed breaking down and the chaos of the dust everywhere, despite all the precautions and plastic sheets that the builders had used. He had finished making the coffee, had removed his tie altogether and tossed it carelessly over the back of one of the kitchen chairs and now faced her across the central isle counter.

'So that would be something you'd have to get used to.'

'Used to? Sorry. I wasn't listening.' She went red and Max did his best to hang on to his temper. Having coerced the woman over his doorstep, using tactics which he had never had to deploy before, he was infuriated to discover that her reaction spoke of the wariness of someone suddenly caught in a trap. She hadn't wanted to come, she didn't care for the fact that she had now found herself here and her forced good manners were threatening to bring out the worst in him.

'I *said*,' he repeated very slowly, 'that saying goodbye to your privacy would be something you would have to get used to.'

'*Saying goodbye to my privacy?* What are you talking about?' She slammed the mug onto the counter surface with shaking hands and some spilt over the sides and slopped onto the counter. 'I may be your secretary, *for the time being*, but that doesn't mean that I have to relinquish my privacy! If those are the kind of demands you've made on the women who have worked for you in the past, then I'm not surprised they left after a few hours!'

'*What* are you talking about?'

In the sudden silence, Vicky realised that he wasn't so much angry at her outburst as perplexed by it. Ah, she thought with a sinking feeling as she realised that whatever his original remark had been she had failed to hear it, absorbed as she had been in her own thoughts.

'What were *you* talking about?' she hedged. She took a long sip of her coffee and eyed him over the rim of the mug.

'If you would make more of an effort to listen to what I'm saying, then you wouldn't fly off the handle because you've caught the tail end and stupidly jumped to the wrong conclusions.'

Vicky bristled at his tone but, since he had a point, she thought it tactful to maintain a discreet silence on the subject.

'I'm sorry,' she said stiffly. 'My mind was miles away.'

'Where? Miles away where?'

He could feel himself itching to launch into an argument, anything to prise something more out of her than secretarial courtesy. True, she lapsed into strong emotion now and again, but then only for the briefest lengths of time and her retreat into that shuttered tower of hers was swift and complete whenever that happened. There was something wary and secretive about her, and his yearning to crack her open like a fruit was beginning to get a little out of control. His sleeping patterns had altered. Often, he would get up for no particular reason at some ungodly hour and even if he did his damnedest to concentrate his whirring mind on business or work or even, God help him, other women, his thoughts would return tirelessly to the small, pale-faced witch facing him now with her cup of coffee, eyes slightly narrowed, like a wild animal that has learnt to be cautious with strangers.

Even more frustrating was the fact that his once ceaseless social life had whittled down to business meetings, client dinners and the occasional meal on his own at the local Italian. The thought of another woman, another of his simple, easy-to-please-just-add-two-tablespoons-of-compliments-and-some-expensive-meals-out women, made him go glassy-eyed with boredom.

He blamed *her*.

'I wasn't thinking of anything in particular,' Vicky said noncommittally, drinking the remainder of her coffee quickly.

Max forced himself to smile, or was it grimace? He couldn't be sure. At any rate, whatever expression emerged felt unnatural.

'The only thing, I've noticed, that gives a woman that abstracted look is the thought of a man.' Fishing. Again. And not very subtly either, he thought. Some of his remarks made him cringe. Where the hell had all his debonair self-assurance gone? He could see her looking at him with a withering expression and his mouth tightened.

'Not *all* women, actually,' Vicky told him politely.

She shoved the empty mug a few inches into the centre of the counter, a little prelude to her request to be driven to the office so that she could collect her car. '*Some* of us do sometimes find our tiny minds cluttered up with something other than thoughts of a man.'

Okay, he thought, I deserved that, but did she have to look quite so…self-righteous? His mind leap frogged into an altogether different tableau, one where self-righteousness played no part, one that involved more emotion than she probably knew how to handle. In fact, a variation on one of the many tableaux that had recently been complicating his previously unfettered life.

'Touché,' he said, flushing darkly. 'Well, I can see that you're ready to go. By the way, that rumour about a supermarket being built near your house—it was just a rumour after all. They've bought a site on the other side of town instead.'

'That's a relief—'

'And, in case you're interested,' Max continued, 'I was talking about the building work you might want to have done on your house at some point. If you're even considering the possibility, I'd suggest you get in touch with Mandy and let her know. Organising all the various people can be a nightmare, even though they all answer to this company.' Who on earth did she think she was kidding? No matter how much she tried to hide it, there was a man somewhere in her life. What he couldn't understand was why she felt compelled to conceal the fact. The mere thought of a man touching that body he constantly fantasised about made him want to grind his teeth.

'You're moving too fast!' she said lightly, walking ahead of him to the front door. She looked over her shoulder and smiled. 'And, from your point of view, I haven't been with the company for two minutes! Shouldn't I have to work a lot longer before I can qualify for any discounted building work from the company?'

God, how he wanted to take that small, delicate face between his hands and crush her mouth with his lips until she couldn't breathe, until every secret was squeezed out of her head. They had stopped at the front door but before she could open it, he leaned against it and stared at her. The tantalising thought that he could just reach out and feel the touch of her lips, run his hands along her smooth neck, made his eyes darken. The prospect of turning fantasy into reality stretched his nerves to breaking point. He could see her pupils dilate as she looked back at him in wordless silence.

'No,' he heard himself say, 'so just set the date.'

She murmured something vague and looked away so that all he could see were her long eyelashes drooping against her cheeks. Her eyelashes, despite the burnished gold of her hair, were dark and thick. He couldn't help himself. He reached out and touched her cheek and she raised her eyes immediately.

'What are you doing?' She flinched back and he abruptly withdrew his hand, which, he was disgusted to see, was shaking from the fleeting contact.

'There was ink on your cheek,' he said smoothly, pushing himself away from the door and opening it for her to precede him out of the house. She rubbed the spot vigorously, not meeting his eyes. 'I want you to type up those letters I dictated in the car today,' he said in a hard voice. His feelings had betrayed him. He had acted as though his body had a mind of its own, and his mouth was tight with anger, at himself and incidentally with her simply for *providing such ludicrous temptation*. 'I'll need them,' he said, opening her door for her and walking around to the driver's seat, 'by lunchtime tomorrow. And cancel my meetings for next Monday. I'll be in New York for three days. Problems with Eva, one of the subsidiaries.' He glanced at her as he pulled out of the drive. 'It would be useful if I had a secretary there.'

'If you like, I can arrange for Tina, Roger's secretary, to accompany you. I know she likes overseas trips.'

His eyes, fixed on the road, were wintry when he answered. 'Leave it. I'll see what can be arranged over there.' And he would bide his time. He had never been a man noted for his patience. He was learning fast.

CHAPTER FIVE

THE following Monday, no sooner had she sat at her desk and switched on the computer terminal than Vicky's internal line buzzed her.

Mandy from Personnel. She had arranged for one of their company architects to have a look at her house and ascertain the cost of any building work needing to be done.

A choking fit ensued as Vicky swallowed a mouthful of coffee down the wrong way, a reaction to her shock at this sudden development.

'Building work?' she asked giddily.

'You mentioned to the big man that you wanted to take advantage of our company policy of subsidised building work for employees?'

'In passing, perhaps…I didn't mean to imply that speed was of the element…'

'You'll learn,' Mandy said dryly from down the end of the telephone. 'Max Forbes doesn't sit on things. He can make a decision in less time than it takes me to make a cup of instant coffee.' There was admiration in her voice. 'And he's obviously decided that your house is in immediate need of repair work. You poor thing. Coming all the way here from Australia to find your house falling about around your ears.'

'Falling about around my ears…?' Vicky repeated in parrot like fashion.

'That's the problem with lodgers,' Mandy continued confidentially. 'My sister rented her house out for a year and it was a mess when she moved back in. Cigarette burns

81

everywhere and the oven had to be chucked out completely. Anyway, Andy Griggs, the architect, is terrific. So...' There was the sound of clicking in the background, 'I'm looking at a week today, twelve-thirty. You can meet with him in your lunch hour, unless you'd rather arrange it for the evening?'

'No!' Vicky said hastily. 'Lunchtime would suit me a lot better!' What was going on? She didn't *want* any building work done to her house! In fact, if her memory served her clearly, she was in the process of trying to tactfully terminate her employment at the company because the smell of trouble was getting stronger with each passing day. 'No, what I mean is...I don't *want*...any building work...'

'I know,' Mandy said sympathetically. Click, click, click. Things were ominously being punched in, in the background. 'Who does? At least you work, so you can be out of the house when they're there. You'll just get back to a sinkful of tea-stained mugs and ladders and work-benches everywhere. So, I've pencilled you in for next Monday. Andy'll meet you at your place, and you shouldn't be longer than an hour...'

'Next Monday.' Her external line was blinking furiously. In ten minutes the post would be delivered and she wouldn't be able to raise her head above water until mid-afternoon at least. She would sort all this building nonsense out later.

Except by the time the thought of architects, builders and Mandy's phone call resurfaced, Vicky was on her way to the childminder to collect Chloe, who was waiting for her with an armful of painting work done at school, which, from experience, Vicky knew would have to be housed at least for a few days until they could be discreetly relegated to the bin.

In her mind, she played guiltily with the thought of bashing the kitchen and the small dining room into one, so that she could have a decent-sized kitchen, big enough for a sensible eating area, maybe even some kind of bar arrangement as well where she could stick a couple of stools. Chloe would like that. It would remind her of the ice-cream bar they'd used to go to once a week in Sydney, where the tall stools were as much of an attraction as the fifty-one different types of ice-cream.

And then, if there was a bit more free wall space, she could have a notice board or two and Chloe's infantile works of art would see the light of day for a bit longer than they did at the moment.

She pushed the nasty, treacherous little thought away and entered into the gist of her daughter's conversation, which today revolved around a stuffed human project in the small class she was attending. Bradley, the name that cropped up most frequently in her daughter's conversation, had apparently hijacked the efforts of the class by accidentally sitting on one of the vital body parts that was destined to be the stuffed figure's head. At this, Chloe laughed until tears came to her eyes and Vicky allowed herself a few moments of unadulterated pleasure, listening to her daughter's uninhibited conversation and bubbling laughter.

'Now we'll have to make a new head,' Chloe confided, 'Miss Jenkins took the buttons off but the smiley mouth took us *ages* to do and we'll have to do a new one.'

'What buttons?'

'The buttons for the *eyes*, Mum!' Chloe said impatiently. 'I'm hungry. What's for tea?'

'Something nourishing and full of goodness,' Vicky said, slowing down to pull into her drive, and her daughter's face fell. She grinned to herself. 'Chicken casserole with potatoes and carrots.'

'Can I have ketchup with it?'

'No reason why not.'

Her thoughts continued to drift like flotsam and jetsam.

The bedrooms. There were the bedrooms. Yes, they were absolutely fine, but really, just say building work *did* take place—which it wouldn't, of course—then wouldn't it be nice to knock a couple of those bedrooms together so that she could have a good-sized room for herself with the luxury of an en suite bathroom? Maybe even a dressing room? Nothing big, but big enough for her to actually see her jumpers and maintain the odd crease-free shirt for work.

And Chloe's room would benefit from having those dated fitted cupboards removed and replaced by a free-standing one in some cheerful, modern colour that her daughter would like.

'I can't eat that many carrots, Mum.'

Vicky glanced down to discover that there was a small mountain of orange on her daughter's plate and she hurriedly rectified the situation and tried to gather her thoughts into a less wayward direction.

In the morning, she would phone Mandy and explain that there had been some hideous mistake, that she wasn't at all interested in having any building work done—at least, not at that moment in time. She would stop letting her thoughts drift in pleasing circles that involved bigger bedrooms and bar counters in kitchens. Instead, she would think of wallpaper, paint effects and possibly getting rid of some of the heavier furniture.

By the following morning, her thoughts had turned full circle and she'd managed to persuade herself that she would meet with the architect after all.

Wouldn't it, she thought reasonably, draw attention to herself if she summarily turned down the whole thing without even assessing the cost? If she met with Andy Griggs, then she could say quite truthfully, no doubt—that it was all going to be too expensive, but that she would consider it at a later date. Who could be suspicious of sensible economic belt-tightening? If she met with the architect, she would also be able to put her mind at rest and find out for herself exactly what could and couldn't be done with the house. She loved the location but she had become accustomed to lighter, airier houses in Australia and she found the closed-in rooms claustrophobic and a little depressing. He might make one or two good suggestions which she could put into practice later on down the road. Once she'd left the company and had saved enough money to do it on her own.

All told, she decided that it was altogether better to go ahead with plans as they stood.

Her carefree frame of mind, now she had persuaded herself that she would see Andy Griggs, gave in fully to the temptation to mentally redesign the house from the bottom brick upwards. She found that there was no aspect of it she couldn't, in her head, alter. She was in high spirits when the telephone shrieked just as she was about to leave work for the day.

The minute she picked up the receiver something told her that Max Forbes would be at the other end. Some inner instinct that sent her pulses racing. It had been peaceful these last two days. Her only communication with her boss had been via e-mail and fax and the work had gone smoothly at this end.

Now, as she heard the deep velvet voice down the end of the line, she realised that something intangible had been missing from the office. Excitement. A certain thrill of anticipation. A heightened state of awareness in which her senses were always, in his presence, on full alert.

'Vicky. Max here. Glad I caught you before you left.'

Vicky played with the cord of the telephone, wondering what could have warranted a phone call when fax and e-mail could easily provide sufficient communication between them and neither sent her nervous system into overdrive.

'How is it going in New York?' she asked politely. 'I've dealt with all your e-mails and sent both of those faxes off to Roger's and Walnut House, as you requested.'

'Yes, yes. Fine. Good. Look, the reason I'm calling is that the problem out here is bigger than I had first thought.' He paused. 'Quite an unpleasant situation has arisen, as a matter of fact.' His voice, when he said that, was cold, and she shivered at the prospect of Max Forbes on the trail of whoever had made the *situation unpleasant*. She had now seen enough of him at work to realise that there was a core of steel running through him that made him a formidable adversary.

'Is there something you'd like me to do from this end?' Vicky asked anxiously.

'For starters, you can cancel my meetings for the next week. Get Anderson to chair the ones that can't wait, but the rest will have to be rescheduled.'

Vicky had already flicked out some notepaper, and even while he spoke was rapidly cataloguing in her head which of his meetings would need to be handed over to Ralph Anderson.

'Anything else?'

'Yes. I need you over here—and that's not a question, it's an order. Heads are going to roll over here and everything will have to be meticulously documented. I'm meeting with lawyers this afternoon to see where we stand, but there's a hell of a lot to get down in writing and a lot of it is highly confidential. I can't trust a temp out here to do the job, provided I can get one to do it well enough, and what's going on is too sensitive for any of the secretaries in the company to deal with the information. I take it,' he said, 'that there won't be a problem with that?'

She could hear the hard edge to the question. He was not going to allow her to wriggle out of this, and however much she told herself that she would clear off as soon as possible, she was reluctant to leave under a black cloud. She needed a good reference if she was to apply for anything worth doing at a later date and clock-watching never got an employee anywhere.

'How long would you need me for?' she asked, heart thudding at the prospect of asking Brenda to have Chloe and her daughter's tears at the thought of her mother going abroad without her. They had never been separated and it was a precedent she had no wish to set.

'Three days at the outside, probably less. Don't worry,' he said coolly, 'I fully appreciate that foreign travel is not something you're interested in, but this time there's no choice. You can book Concorde over. You know where I'm staying. Get a room there as well. I'll make sure there's no problem in that area.'

Vicky sighed inaudibly. 'Will that be all?'

'E-mail me with your time of arrival and expect to be working the minute your feet touch the ground.'

'Of course,' she said with a hint of sarcasm. 'I wouldn't dare expect otherwise.'

The adrenaline was still surging through her bloodstream when, one hour later, she found herself asking Brenda whether she could keep Chloe for the following night, at the most two.

'I'll pay you, of course,' she said, over a cup of coffee, and Brenda looked at her intently.

'Never you mind the money, Vicky. Just so long as this job doesn't start taking over your life. I've seen some of these career women and they spend their lives in a state of permanent exhaustion. Not,' she added thoughtfully, 'that it seems to be doing you any harm at all.'

'What do you mean?' In the corner of the room Chloe and Brenda's little girl Alice, who was one year older, were playing a vigorous game of Barbies. From the sidelines, Ken watched with blank-eyed interest.

'I haven't seen you look so…so *well*…for months. Skin radiant, eyes sparkling. Whatever work this boss is feeding you, it agrees with your system.'

'He's *feeding me*?' Vicky said, laughing, half at the antics of the Barbie dolls, who now appeared to be engaged in physical warfare despite their attire of bikinis and high-heeled pumps, and half at Brenda's mistaken notions. 'Too much work, heaps of responsibility and no end of sarcastic comments, not to mention nosy prying and pointed innuendoes.'

Brenda laughed in response. 'Well, watch out. A girl could get addicted to a diet like that.'

But it was settled, as was the flight to New York which she'd booked that afternoon, and she felt the first stirrings of excitement when she arrived at Heathrow with her small flight bag and was shown all the respect and subservience obviously given to anyone who had enough money to fly by the most expensive method in the world.

Only when she booked into the hotel in New York, after an enjoyable and uneventful flight in surroundings that were speedy but cramped, did the excitement give way to apprehension.

It dawned on her more fully now that she was going to

be here with Max Forbes for at least two days, maybe three, and this time there would be no five o'clock ending and eight-thirty start.

He had arranged to meet her in the hotel bar, to brief her on what was going on, and she felt a tremor of nerves as she slipped on her smart oatmeal-coloured trouser suit, with a long-sleeved cream polo top underneath the tailored jacket, and bundled her hair into some form of chignon. The person staring back at her in the mirror looked impeccably professional but still managed to give the impression that the wearer of those smart clothes might well have been happier in a pair of jeans and an oversized shirt.

He was already there and waiting for her when she walked into the bar. She spotted him immediately at a table in the corner, swirling a drink around in one hand. She hadn't seen him look so tired before. As if to confirm the impression, he rubbed his eyes wearily with his thumbs before asking her what she wanted to drink and summoning across a waiter to take the order.

'You look awful,' Vicky blurted out, and he smiled with wry amusement.

'And it's very nice to see you too. Glad you could make it. Did you have to do a lot of rearranging?'

'I managed.' She shrugged and sat back to allow the waiter to place her glass of cold white wine in front of her. 'What's going on? Would you like to brief me now or would you rather we wait until morning, when I'll have my laptop and can take more substantial notes?'

She sipped some of her wine and felt herself relax fractionally.

'No, I'll give you the lowdown now. Have you eaten, by the way?' He didn't give her time to answer. Instead, he beckoned the waiter across and told him to bring two of the prawn salads and some bread. 'To cut a long story short, a few days ago I received a rather disturbing call from one of my accountants for Eva. To give you a bit of background, Eva's one of the smaller subsidiaries which my father took a personal interest in because it dealt with his hobby-horse, namely computer games. As you know, computer games have come a long way and Eva's profits have risen steadily and fairly dramatically over the past five years.' He gulped back a mouthful of his drink and then banged his glass on the table, as though giving vent to some frustrating but powerful emotion. 'In the past year, sizeable amounts have, apparently, gone missing. It transpires that the chairman of the company, a man I have known for years, has been slowly but surely embezzling money in the form of bogus clients, forged signatures, etc, etc.' He rubbed his eyes tiredly again and then leaned heavily back into his chair and half closed his eyes. 'I've spent the past two days locked up in a room with the accountant, and today three high-powered lawyers, working out how to deal with the problem. So far, he's unaware. We feel that our best bet is to surprise him with the evidence, just in case he attempts to tamper with it and add to his crimes.'

'Will he go to prison?' Vicky was horrified.

'I don't know,' Max said simply. 'Fraud deserves punishment but, if he's sacked, then that will be punishment enough as far as I'm concerned. He'll be forced to take early retirement and his reputation within the computer industry will be over. Aside from that,' he sighed, 'he has a family. I'm godfather to one of his children!' He sat back as food was brought to their table. Typically, there was lots of it, and it was clearly of restaurant standard, despite the fact that they were in the hotel bar. 'It's a bloody nightmare, but you understand why it was imperative that an external secretary was brought in to deal with what's going on. It's not a big company and tongues wag.' They both dug into their salads. The prawns were as large as crabs and there was enough salad on the oversized plates to satisfy the most ravenous of appetites. 'The fewer people who know about this, the more successful our damage limitation will be. In a field like this, shares could fall at the merest mention of wrong-doing.'

'So what will you do?'

'What do you think I should do?'

'Don't tell me you would take the opinion of a lowly secretary seriously,' she said in an attempt to defuse his mood, although his reply was unexpectedly serious.

'I'm always ready to listen to suggestions.' His tone of voice left no doubt as to his sincerity.

'Well.' She paused and considered what she had been told. 'He would obviously have to leave immediately, and someone would have to ensure that his career would be effectively over. You're right, fraud would be punishable by a long prison stretch. But if I knew this man's family, I suppose I would be tempted to dismiss him with all the necessary warnings and look on it as a salutary experience.'

'Very soft-hearted.'

'Only when it comes to certain things,' Vicky informed him briefly.

'Care to tell me what brings out the hard edge in you?'

'No.' She could feel his eyes roving over her as she bent to concentrate on her salad. 'What is the format for tomorrow?' As a conversation-stopper it was obvious, but it worked. The remaining hour was spent discussing various aspects of the problem and what would be expected of her in terms of her work. By the time she left to head back up to her room, she felt exhausted. Her head was spinning from the permutations of the problem confronting them, and she was uneasily aware that with this trip to New York she was taking yet another step towards being enmeshed in a job she knew could not last.

The following two days were the most invigorating and exciting of her career. Fact had proved stranger than fiction, as it usually does. The man involved in the embezzlement was not quite the cold-blooded fraudster she had expected. When summoned into the boardroom before lawyers and two independent accountants, he quickly confessed everything.

Sitting in the background, her fingers flew over her notepad as she took down everything that was said in her impeccable shorthand—a dying skill for which she was now immeasurably grateful. Although he was speaking into a tape recorder, she didn't think that she could bear to transcribe the emotional breakdown from a tape.

Harry Shoring wept—loud, wrenching sobs born of guilt, fear and remorse.

He had, he confessed, originally seen the embezzlement as a stop-gap measure. He had intended to pay back every penny of what he'd taken but the whole thing had snowballed. His daughter, it turned out, had been involved in a car accident and the insurance had gone only so far to covering the cost of the surgery and the hospitals, but more had needed doing. Much, much more, or else his child would have been left a cripple for the rest of her life. He'd faced the prospect of forking out for radical new treatment which might restore the use of her legs and, when his own money had run out, he'd turned to the company for what he had seen would be a loan. A loan no one else knew about.

Throughout the long hours spent listening to his account, Max sat in silence, asking only the briefest of questions, even though it was to him that Harry's watery eyes most frequently turned. His face betrayed nothing whatsoever. He made no notes whatsoever, leaving that to the rest of the assembled crew, but she had no doubt that every single word spoken was being absorbed and dealt with by that sharp, clever mind of his.

By the end of the second day, and after some discussions with the accountant and the chief lawyer, Harry Shoring was told that he would not face the prospect of a prison sentence. Max would, he said himself, repay every penny of the debt from his own personal fortune, an offer which was met with a gasp of gratitude from the older man, but in return Harry would have to leave the firm immediately and his pension would be altered to compensate for the embezzlement.

'What about Jessie?' he asked tearfully. 'She's been coming along so well...my poor little baby...only fourteen...'

'I'll make sure that all health costs are covered until progress is complete.'

The solution was unbelievably generous and compassionate, Vicky thought two hours later as she sat in the hotel conference room putting the finishing touches to various bits of documentation that would require signatures.

Her mind played back Max's words and expressions over those past two days and something strong and disturbing quivered inside her. A confusing and uninvited notion that her secrecy about Chloe was somehow an act of betrayal, that she should tell him about her daughter. Hadn't she seen enough of him now to know that he wouldn't abuse the knowledge? The thought hovered above her like a storm cloud filled with threat. The temptation to blurt it all out was very nearly irresistible, but something held her back. Thick, sluggish fear, lodged inside her like a vice, stilled the little voice, reasoned to her that any confession, in the short term, would ruin this important trip to New York, told her to keep her dangerous secret to herself. After all, her daughter played no part in her working life and never would. He would never find out, not if she remained careful. And wasn't the old adage *better safe than sorry* the most priceless of advice? She ignored her gut feeling that her reasoning was built on very shaky foundations and stifled her inner protests.

Instead, she finished her stack of typing and breathed a sigh of relief. Tomorrow she would be catching the day flight back to Heathrow and would be in time to collect Chloe from school. They had spoken twice a day and she'd been amused to discover that her daughter had not spent hours sobbing over her mother's absence. Chloe, she thought, was growing up. She'd missed her daughter, but Vicky had to admit that the past two days had been rather wonderful. The fleeting window of freedom had made her see how difficult her life had been as a single-parent family. She'd forgotten what it was like to have a night of undisturbed sleep and to awaken in the morning without having to plunge into insistent childish conversation. For a few seconds, she thought how wonderful it must be to have help in the form of a partner. In her own head, Vicky had equated partnership with the likes of Shaun, but now she thought that four hands, two heads and the security of sharing must be rather nice.

She wondered what kind of father Max would make and, in the solitude of the enormous conference room, she flushed and glanced around her, as though afraid that unseen eyes might pick a hole in her head and yank out the wayward thought.

She was so consumed by the uninvited image that when she heard his voice from the door, she imagined, for a couple of seconds, that she must be dreaming, but when she turned around he was lounging in the doorframe, casually dressed in a pair of olive-green trousers and a short-sleeved shirt that emphasised his superb build.

'I've just finished,' Vicky said, in case he'd come to find out why she was taking so long. There had been a lot more to type out than she had first expected.

'Good. In that case you can run along and have a bath, get on your glad rags and join me for dinner.' He smiled slowly at her and raked his fingers through his hair. 'Unless you have other plans?'

'No other plans,' Vicky mumbled, switching off the computer and making a big deal of rustling her bits of paper to hide her confusion. He continued to lounge oppressively by the door, watching her antics, which made her feel like a gerbil pointlessly gadding about on a wheel in a cage.

'I'll meet you in the bar in—' he glanced down at his watch '—forty minutes, and we'll take a cab to the restaurant.'

'With everyone else?'

'Everyone else has a family to go home to,' Max said drily, 'and after the hours they've put in over the past few days, they'll be only too glad to get back to a bit of normality. Just you and me to celebrate the best outcome that could have been achieved, given the circumstances.'

At which he gave her a mocking half salute and departed, leaving Vicky to hastily gather her paperwork, dash up to her bedroom, have a quick bath and then devote the remainder of the time left to surveying her wardrobe, which was scantily inadequate.

She finally appeared in the hotel bar ten minutes late in a pair of black trousers, the other half of her one and only trouser suit, and a beige long-sleeved woollen top which had been flung in her case as an afterthought, and for which she was now grateful as the other three tops she had brought with her were suitable for work only. They were businesslike shirts, smartly tailored and ludicrously inappropriate for doing anything apart from sitting in front of a computer or taking notes at meetings.

Max was waiting for her in the bar. He saw her before she saw him and had a few seconds during which he appreciatively took in the trousers, her slim hips and waist and the top which fitted like a glove. He still found it incredible that she could do this to him, make him feel like a teenager all over again, but he was accepting it in the manner of someone accepting the inexplicable but unavoidable. He was even, he realised, becoming tuned in to her thoughts from the changing expressions on her face. Over the past two days he had found himself watching her, knowing when she agreed with what was being said and when she didn't. More amazingly, he had begun unconsciously looking to her for approval of some of his decisions, although he wasn't about to heed the advice of any woman or be swayed in his thoughts simply because of the way Vicky's eyes shifted to him, or the way her mouth tightened in unspoken disagreement.

He could feel that shadow of anxiety hovering around her as they left the hotel bar and headed for the restaurant. It was one of his favourites. Upbeat and stylish with classy food but without the accompanying atmosphere of snobbish elitism that so many restaurants liked to cultivate. Unlike all the women he had dated in the past, she would not be impressed by a stuffy, expensive, snobbish place. She would wrinkle that small, perfect nose in mild distaste even though she wouldn't make any comment. And why not admit it, he thought, he wanted to impress her. He wanted to show her what a well-travelled, worldly-wise, sophisticated yet unpretentious kind of guy he was.

Which meant putting her at ease. Which meant, he thought with the usual frustration he felt when he was alone with her, talking about work. Which was no problem, and over the superb starters they chatted about the outcome of the fraud fiasco. Harry Shoring, spared the prospect of prison, had been weak with gratitude, and had agreed to leave the company immediately with his reputation intact although only so long as he took early retirement and remained retired. Any hint of his recommencing work in another company and, Max had said, he would have no alternative but to spill the beans.

'Are you pleased?' Vicky asked, finishing her cold white wine and allowing her glass to be refilled.

'We couldn't have been more understanding,' Max said bluntly.

'*You* couldn't have been more understanding. After all, you *will* be virtually taking over as his financial backbone until medical treatment on his daughter can't go any further.'

Max, seeing the frank and open admiration on her face, didn't know whether to feel flattered or impatient. The generous gesture had been made without thinking. His father's friend, whatever he had done, had a sick child and was broke. Max had money—*not* helping Harry was not an alternative. No, he didn't want her admiration for his altruistic gesture. He wanted much, much more than that, and right now he was a million miles away from it. But at least she had shed that air of nervous suspicion, even if, he suspected with wry self-irony, it was the wine rather than his witty, seamless conversation that was responsible.

'It was nothing,' Max said with a dismissive shrug of his broad shoulders.

'Oh, but it *is*,' she insisted, watching as he topped up her glass. 'It may be nothing to *you*, but lots of men would have just turned their backs and walked away from the situation without feeling any sense of responsibility.'

Adulation for a simple act of humanity, he wanted to tell her, was *not* what he was after. Her cheeks were beginning to look a little flushed, and he saw, with some surprise, that most of the second bottle of wine he had ordered had gone and she was now toying with the food on her plate. She had shoved the few remaining bits of vegetables into a face-like shape, which made him grin to himself, because there was something endearingly childlike about it when her approach to life was always so coolly efficient and businesslike.

'Nice face,' he remarked gravely. 'Anyone in particular?' He tilted his head to one side in a question and tried not to burst out laughing when she went bright red and hurriedly closed her knife and fork, looking around her to see whether anyone had been observing her little activity.

'Perhaps we ought to leave,' he suggested. 'And don't look so tortured.' He leaned forward and whispered conspiratorially, '*No one was watching you. It's not that kind of place.*' When she smiled sheepishly back at him, he felt his heart do something odd and his breathing thickened slightly.

They had to get out of here. She was driving him crazy. He couldn't wait to pay the bill, leaving an outrageously generous tip because he couldn't wait for the head waiter to find him some change, and he was so excruciatingly aware of her sitting next to him in the cab that he could almost feel his skin tingling. She'd had too much to drink and the effect was devastating to his senses.

'Oh, walk with me to my room,' she sighed, supporting herself on his arm when he attempted to point her in the direction of the elevator, mumbling something about having one last drink on his own at the bar before retiring.

She'd braided her hair into a French plait and she played with it as it hung over one shoulder.

'Okay,' he said reluctantly, 'but you should get a good night's sleep. You must be exhausted.'

Her eyes danced. 'Never felt livelier.' Her hand, he noticed as they rode the elevator to her floor in silence, was still on his arm, a slight but insistent pressure that was having a noticeable effect on his body parts, one in particular.

He virtually pulled her to her room, watching as she fumbled with the credit card-style key and finally removing it from her and opening the door himself, then he stood politely back so that she could enter. Enter and turn to face him.

'I had a fantastic evening,' she breathed, looking at him then walking through into the small sitting room of the bedroom suite so that he inevitably followed. She turned abruptly and approached him. 'Did you?'

'Fantastic.' He cleared his voice.

'Then why do you look so edgy?' she teased.

Her lips were still curved into a smile when he bent his head and covered them with his own. It was like tasting nectar for the first time and after a moment's pause, she returned his kiss. Returned it with all the passion he was feeling himself, arching her body into his, pressing so that she could be in no doubt as to the urgency of his response.

He groaned hoarsely. Somehow they found themselves to the sofa. Her breasts. He had to see them, taste them, lick them. He wanted to touch every inch of the body that had filled his mind for longer than he cared to think.

When she pulled up her jumper, exposing her small, ripe breasts with their erotic lace covering, he drew his breath in sharply. Through the lace, he could see the pink, protruding tip of her nipple and he licked it, but the delicacy of this was too much for him. He felt as though he couldn't wait.

With urgent hands, he tugged the bra down so that her breasts spilled out, small, firm breasts with big nipples that were dark and engorged.

With a moan, she pushed his head down and he could feel her body shudder as he suckled at one, then the other, taking as much of her into his mouth as he could while his feverish hands prised open her legs and massaged her thighs.

Another time, he thought, and there *would* be another, he would take his time, turn lovemaking into a work of art. But for now, he was too explosively hungry for her to wait.

CHAPTER SIX

VICKY made very sure that she was out of her office when Max returned to work after New York. She knew that he would be coming in to the office at nine-thirty because of the e-mail he'd sent her the previous day. Nevertheless, from the cowardly sanctuary of the Ladies, she could still feel her heart thumping at a mile a minute.

She would give him fifteen minutes, a never-ending stretch of time during which she pointlessly stared at her reflection in the mirror and attempted to look busy with a make-up compact, just in case someone else entered the large, plush cloakroom and wondered what small, red-haired Vicky Lockhart was doing there, her cheeks flushed with colour, her eyes over-bright. It was a relatively small, friendly company, and during the short space of time that she'd been working there she could say with reasonable accuracy that she was on nodding acquaintance with most of the staff. If anyone came upon her now, staring sightlessly in the mirror, hands shaking, lips dry and an expression of gut-wrenching dread on her face, they would rush her to the nearest hospital. Or, at any rate, the nearest Sanatorium. At the very least, they would ask lots of concerned, prying questions for which she had no answers.

She only knew that her mind had spent the past few days preoccupied with one thing and one thing only.

Or perhaps *one person* would be more to the point.

When she thought of Max Forbes, her brain seemed to close down completely, leaving her at the cruel whim of memories that made her body begin to ache.

She gripped the chrome tap and stared hard and purposefully into the sink, willing the onslaught of thoughts to go away, but it was no good.

The worst, most humiliating thought of all was the realisation that none of it would have happened if she had not invited him into her bedroom. True, she'd had more than her usual amount to drink, but she knew, inside herself, that blaming a few glasses of wine for what had happened between them would be an act of cowardice. The plain, unadorned truth was that she had felt relaxed enough with him in that restaurant to open up. She'd stopped putting up barriers and had succumbed to the power of his raw masculinity and the sexy charm that she'd fought desperately against from the very first minute she'd laid eyes on him.

She turned on the tap and rinsed her face with ice-cold water, but beneath the water she could still feel her cheeks burning. Not only had she proceeded to force the man into her room, or at least put him in a position where to say goodnight and leave would risk appearing rude, she'd then done the unthinkable.

Her body had been on fire. During the meal, she'd felt herself get more and more turned on every time his eyes fell on her. By the time they'd reached her bedroom, her imagination had been in full flow and she'd been in no mood to put the brakes on.

She'd felt sexy and alluring and vampish. The memory of it was enough to make her shudder with mortification. Amazing what a few glasses of good wine and an active imagination could do to a girl, she now thought bitterly. She had slowly begun to pull up her jumper, her fingers playing with the soft fabric, while he'd stood in silence and watched, his eyes dark with desire at what she was so readily and eagerly offering him. No strings attached. On a plate. With a silver spoon. And all condiments included. What man wouldn't have been burning up with enthusiasm for such an abandoned offering? She'd opened the floodgates by kissing him, and doing a strip tease, in a ridiculously sensuous fashion which had probably had him sniggering all the way back to his bedroom.

But he hadn't been sniggering then. She'd seen the darkening intent in his eyes with a flare of wild excitement. When their mouths had met, she'd felt as though the moment had been one she'd been waiting for all her life and the greed of his responses had fuelled in her a heady sense of power. When he'd pulled down her bra, the air had felt wonderfully cool on her hot skin and her nipples had puckered in response and pulling back had been out of the question. She had, and the thought of it now made her groan with shame, shoved him down to her breasts. There had been just one thing in her head at that point, and that was the burning need to have her desire sated. She *needed* to feel his mouth on her nipples, sucking, drawing them in, nibbling and licking the pulsing, protruding bud.

Her legs, opened and waiting for his urgent exploring hand, had been a wet cavern of delight. He'd massaged her thighs while she had placed both her hands behind her head, eyes shut, body arched upwards to receive his ravaging mouth.

From outside, the light had filtered into the room and spread an interesting array of shadows around them, so that everything seemed other-worldly. She could remember watching in drugged fascination as he'd stripped off his clothes. His hands hadn't been able to undo his shirt-buttons quickly enough and in the end, he had ripped it off. Only a few hours before, he'd been the archetypal boss with his demure, efficient secretary. She'd taken notes, her legs neatly crossed beneath the prim, unrevealing skirt. No one would ever have guessed that only a few hours later she would have shed all her inhibitions and thrown herself at her boss with the urgency and feverish passion of a woman who had spent her entire adult life in a sexual desert.

Vicky inspected her face in the bathroom mirror for guilt and shame. She would have to make sure that she eliminated both before she ventured back into her office. She'd made an utter fool of herself but she wasn't about to lose every shred of dignity in the process.

She would have to make a show of pretending that the whole sorry episode had not made any indelible mark on her. She smiled ruefully at her reflection at the thought of that whopping lie. The fact was that her moment of abandon had cost her dearly. She straightened, fished into the make-up compact and began applying a little mascara, controlling her shaking fingers with effort.

Even in the throes of her love affair with Shaun, before revulsion had set in, she'd never felt such a burst of dangerous, white-hot craving. She'd not been able to get enough of Max. When his mouth had left her breasts and moistly made its way down the flat planes of her stomach, the throbbing between her legs had made her squirm. The first touch of his tongue flicking gently at her pulsing womanhood had made her moan loudly and thrash against the bed, then she'd begun to move against his mouth, her body twisting up and down and from side to side while he gripped her hips and plunged his tongue deeper and deeper into her welcoming, honey-sweet essence. Her orgasm had been a wild, shuddering release that had seemed to vibrate into infinity, and still their lovemaking had continued. He'd waited for her body to sag then, slowly but surely, like a maestro fine-tuning an instrument, he'd aroused her all over again, and this time she'd been the one to explore his body, until his desperate need for her had made him push her down onto his huge erection.

At no point and at all points, they could have stopped themselves from reaching the final destination.

But they hadn't and there was no point killing herself with regrets. It had happened and now she would just have to suffer the consequences.

She finished with the mascara, and dabbed a little lipstick on. Blusher she would leave. There was enough natural colour in her cheeks to make anyone think she had overdone it with the artificial stuff anyway.

She was stuffing the compact into her bag and wondering whether she should head back, when the cloakroom door was pushed open and Catherine, secretary to one of the company directors, let out a little squeal of relief.

'I've been looking for you *everywhere*,' she said anxiously. 'What on earth have you *done to him*?'

'*Done* to him? Done to *whom*?' Vicky said, feigning ignorance.

'Your boss! He got in ten minutes ago and stormed into Jeremy's office like a tiger in need of a victim, then he ordered me to *smoke you out*. Those were his precise words, Vicky. *Smoke you out*.' The excitement of what could possibly be going on had replaced the urgency of her mission. Catherine now looked as though she would be more than willing to listen to any number of juicy explanations, however impatient Max had been to get hold of Vicky. '*So what's going on?* I haven't seen him that thunderous for…forever, and *I've* been here since the company got going! *What* have you gone and done?'

'I'd better go, Catherine. No point *you* getting into trouble as well by staying here too long.' Which did the trick. Catherine jumped and practically shoved Vicky out of the cloakroom so that she found herself propelled into her office with a lot less preparation time than she had hoped for.

Forbiddingly, he was waiting for her in his office, and the dividing door was open so that she was subjected to the full force of his scowling face as he beckoned her into the chair in front of his desk. Vicky sat down, crossed her legs and adopted a bland expression. At least, that was what she'd aimed for. Her mouth felt as though the muscles had seized up, which probably meant that she was displaying something more akin to a deranged grimace.

'What's *this* all about?' He held a sheet of paper in one hand, which he then proceeded to dangle dismissively before letting it flutter down to the desk. Vicky followed its progress downwards, mesmerised, before finding her voice.

'I thought it best… I realise that…I'm afraid that due to my own stupidity…' She didn't dare look him directly in the eyes so instead she shifted her focus to an indeterminate point somewhere beyond his left shoulder. He'd tilted his head to one side and now appeared to be settling down to wait for her to finish her sentence.

'I just think that what happened in New York has jeopardised my position here, that's all,' she concluded, when she realised that she was going to find no help whatsoever from his quarter. He began drumming his fingers on the desk, an aggravating, steady sound that did nothing for her already shredded nerves.

'And don't act as though you don't know what I'm talking about!' she muttered when he still hadn't said anything. 'I don't think that a boss-secretary relationship is feasible when the boss has slept with the secretary! Do you?' Or even, she thought guiltily, when the secretary has slept with the boss. The steadily drumming fingers slowed their rhythm without actually stopping. The sound was driving her mad.

'It happened,' he said softly, leaning back into the chair and folding his hands behind his head so that he could stare at her through narrowed eyes. 'These things do, believe it or not. People have too much to drink...'

'I knew it! You're blaming me! I wondered when you would get down to that.'

'I wasn't blaming *anyone*. I was merely saying that human nature is not always strong. We both made a mistake—' he paused, allowing her to digest that '—but that doesn't mean that we have to let one slip-up throw everything out of proportion. Unless, of course, you feel that you wouldn't be able to put the incident behind you...in which case, I would more than understand if you walked out of this office right now.'

'What do you mean, *not able to put the incident behind me*?' Vicky asked suspiciously.

'I'm merely saying that you may feel yourself more involved with me than you care to admit...'

Vicky emitted a shriek of near-hysterical laughter which she hoped was sufficient to inform him of the absurdity of his suggestion. In case it wasn't, she clarified coldly, 'It was a mistake, as you said. Nothing more.'

'So where's the problem? We put it behind us, we get on with life. I don't want to lose a brilliant secretary and I don't suppose you're that willing to throw away a damn good pay packet, so let's make a deal. We put it down to experience and it's never mentioned again. Believe me, I feel as exposed as you do. I don't approve of any boss having sex with his secretary and, aside from that, I opened myself up to any number of scenarios which I'm experienced enough to spot and avoid. What if you'd cried *sexual harassment*? It's a measure of my trust in you and my belief that we can carry on working together that I'm asking you to stay at all.'

'And what if we find that it doesn't work that way?' She noticed that he hadn't even euphemistically used the phrase *making love*. They had *had sex*: regrettable, but not earth-shattering.

'If it doesn't work that way, then...' He shrugged and fixed his cool, grey eyes on her. 'We call it a day.'

Choosing between the devil and the deep blue sea were equally unimpressive options, she was fast discovering.

Walking out would tell its own story. And what if he got it into his head to follow her? If only because of the secretarial skills she knew he valued? He obviously had no qualms about just *showing up* on her doorstep. What if he just *showed up* and Chloe happened to be around?

On the other hand, to remain was to open a Pandora's box. Making love to Max had stirred her emotions into a chaotic, seething mass. She didn't know what she felt, she just knew that fear was involved—and not just fear of what Max could do to her should he ever find out the truth of her situation, but fear of what she could do to herself simply by spending time with him. She was finding it easier and easier to let her defences slip. One day she would make a fatal error.

'I'll give it a couple of weeks,' she said now, sitting on the fence because she couldn't think of where else to go. 'But I'll only stay on one condition,' she continued inflexibly, 'and the condition is that if I decide, for whatever reason, that I'm unable to work for you, then you leave me alone. You don't try and persuade me to stay, you just respect my decision.'

'Of course,' Max said, magnanimous in victory. He felt himself sag with relief. He hadn't known what he would do if she'd stuck to her decision to resign. In fact, it was true to say that he hadn't known a number of things until she'd come along and turned his world upside down, because there was no use pretending otherwise. He felt like a man clinging onto a piece of driftwood in the middle of a stormy sea, with no real clue as to where he was going or when his ordeal would end.

'Fine,' she said quietly, looking away from him while he continued to stare at her. He wondered how much or how little their lovemaking had meant to her. Certainly, her averted profile wasn't giving much away, and he was overcome by a primal urge to force her to submit to him, to confess that he had made the earth move for her, to acknowledge that she'd never been as aroused by anyone in her life as she'd been aroused by him. In fact, he was assailed by a ridiculous, puerile desire to hear her tell him that he was the best.

He irritably began tapping his fountain pen on the desk, while his mind threw its leash and travelled joyously down memory lane, rearing up at the volcanic turn-on the sight of her naked body had been for him. Every bit of her uncovered had been a revelation without compare. The taste of her nipples still lingered on his tongue, making him feel worryingly unsteady. Sleeping with her, instead of diminishing his fantasies, had succeeded in making them proliferate. Right now, at this very moment, he could quite easily have locked the outside office door, whatever the hell anyone who came along might think, and taken her. Stripped her of her neat little grey outfit, a libido-quencher of the highest order, and laid her on his desk, naked and exquisitely open to his mouth and hands. He would have liked to have suckled on her delicious breasts at this very moment, with the fax machine going outside, the light on his phone informing him that he'd calls waiting and the computer terminal begging to be downloaded of its important messages. He couldn't think of anything more erotic than letting the world of high finance wait until their needs were satisfied. He cleared his throat and hastily rummaged pointlessly through some of the paperwork lying in his open briefcase. With great effort, he managed to get his mind to operate on a more relevant level and, with even greater effort, he succeeded in speaking to her about work and what had been happening in the office since he had been away.

She was leaving when he thought to ask, 'What did Andy Griggs have to say about your house?'

Vicky, with one hand on the doorknob, turned to face him. Andy Griggs had slipped her mind. 'I'm seeing him this evening. I had to cancel our previous appointment,' she said, 'but of course I shan't go ahead with anything, not until I know one way or another...'

Max felt an unsteadying combination of impotence, panic and anger. 'Naturally,' he said calmly, making himself smile and giving a rueful but utterly understanding shrug of his broad shoulders. 'Have you decided what you would like to have done anyway?'

'Well...' Vicky hesitated. 'I...I *have* noticed, ever since this all came up, that the house is in desperate need of renovation. I never gave it much thought when I first got back to England. I was too busy sorting out other aspects of my life. But last weekend I had a walk around the place and—' she sighed '—things need changing. The rooms need rearranging. It worked when it was rented out because most of the time the tenants were students, so four small bedrooms was an attraction, but now I think I'd like to make the master bedroom much bigger, perhaps with a little sitting area, and I could do something about having a pl—' She'd very nearly said *playroom*, but in time she swallowed the word down, although the near-slip had jolted her. 'A place to work. I could put my computer in there...' She gave her head a little shake and smiled apologetically. She hadn't meant to say so much. As usual, she had ended up rambling on. 'I have no idea why I'm planning all this,' she said firmly, 'There's a good chance I won't remain with the company—' she looked down when she said that, because the reasons for her departure were close enough to the surface of her mind to make her tremble '—and, even if I do, I haven't got the money.'

'Money isn't a problem.'

'Not for you perhaps.' She pulled open the door, not wanting to become embroiled in a conversation that was only serving to remind her of yet something else she would be giving up when she left. 'Will that be all? I think I should be able to cover most of this by this afternoon and the rest I'll do first thing in the morning, if that's all right with you.'

'Fine. I'll be out of the office this afternoon.' He paused. 'I take it there won't be any surprises waiting for me tomorrow morning when I get in?'

Vicky flushed but didn't say anything and, after a few seconds, he gave her a curt nod of the head, which she read as her dismissal, and she went back into her office, breathing a sigh of relief that she was out of his presence, even though things had not gone according to plan. The plan had *been* that she would now be on her way to yet another employment agency, clutching her CV and prepared to do a typing test. Instead, here she still was, ensconced in her leather swivel chair, and she was edgily aware that a part of her was relieved that she wouldn't be leaving. It was, in fact, the same part that had encouraged her to remove her jumper a few nights previously and to offer herself to the man she kept reminding herself she needed to escape from. And it was the same part that responded to his wit, his humour, the part that had, she acknowledged shakily, become addicted to his every mood, every shift in his expression, every change in his voice. Her fingers continued to fly across the computer keys and her eyes scanned the document she was typing, but her mind played its dangerous games somewhere else. Somewhere in a land of No Return, where her heart seemed to have wandered when she wasn't looking.

She was so absorbed in her thoughts that she jumped when he strode into her section an hour later, slinging on his jacket and checking his pockets in an unconscious and automatic gesture which she had grown to expect. She stopped with her hands hovering fractionally over the keyboard. She could feel nervous perspiration prickling under her arms and above her lip. She even thought she could feel the rush of blood through her veins. Hot, boiling blood, surging like a toxin. She'd fallen in love with him and it was like feeding off poison. He had to repeat three times that he would see her in the morning before she came to her senses and nodded, not daring to open her mouth because she knew her voice would give her away. Her eyes drank him up, though. She felt like a guilty sinner, gorging on temptation as she took in the lean hungry power of his body—the body she had touched!—the angles of his face, the full, sensual lower lip that promised so much more than fulfilling sex.

When the door slammed behind him, she could feel her body slump, and it was blessed relief to finally leave the office at a little before five so that she could rush to her daughter and try and regain some of her lost sanity. Chloe would be a tonic, with her incessant chatter and her innocent preoccupation with her school day. It wouldn't leave room in her head for Max.

Unfortunately thoughts of him plagued her all through

her daughter's tea, and by the time she had settled Chloe upstairs and opened the door to the architect she felt wrung out.

It didn't help that the expression on his face as he was shown through the house made her realise, dejectedly, that the house really *was* in need of a serious overhaul and that it was now out of the question that any such overhaul would be forthcoming.

'You do realise,' he said thoughtfully, rocking on his heels and tapping his lips with his pen, 'that you have damp.' He led her across to one of the offending walls in the sitting room, fiddled around with a gadget and then held it up for her to see. 'If something isn't done about it fairly soon, the walls are going to deteriorate. Your idea about knocking through a couple of rooms would be a good way of clearing up the problem because we can do some damp-proofing at the same time.' Over a cup of coffee, he continued to elaborate on her ideas, tossing in more enticing ones of his own, which Vicky listened to with a sinking heart.

'I haven't got money for all of that,' she finally confessed bluntly. 'I mean, I might just have to do a superficial job, at least for the time being. A paint job here and there, some wallpaper, maybe get some new furniture.'

'Won't take care of the damp.'

'Well, what can you do about that?' She frowned irritably, thinking that she hadn't eaten her dinner as yet and her stomach was beginning to feel hollow. 'You must be able to patch it up somehow.'

'Patch-up jobs never really do the trick,' he said gently. For an earnest, middle-aged architect he certainly had a winning salesman's technique, she thought drily.

'Well, I shall think about everything you've said.'

'And I'll send my detailed report through shortly,' he

told her, getting to his feet and handing her the cup of coffee. 'I say go the whole way,' he advised, walking ahead of her to the front door and throwing one last professional and withering glance around the hall. 'It'll cost you a fraction of what you would have to pay if you looked outside the company, and you wouldn't have to wait months before work could begin.'

Vicky opened the door swiftly before she could be further undermined by this subversive talk.

'In fact,' he said, pausing to look at her thoughtfully, 'I've been told that the go-ahead for this particular project could be as early as next week. Just think, in less than four weeks you could turn this into the house of your dreams.' The brown eyes crinkled at her and she laughed.

'Go away before you win me over completely! I'll think about it.'

Which she did, as she made herself some beans on toast and untied her hair, running her fingers through its length, idly thinking that she really ought to go and get it all chopped off into a tailored hairstyle more suitable for a mum.

Andy Griggs did a good line in persuasion, she thought. He hadn't been pushy, but his assessment of the house and what it needed had been professional and honest. It was hardly his fault that some of his suggestions were so tempting that she had to stop herself salivating at the mouth at the thought of them. At one point, he'd even managed to persuade her that altering her staircase completely would transform the overall aspect of the house, and she'd inanely found herself agreeing. He would send his detailed analysis through, she thought, and she would promptly put it somewhere safe and out of sight. In a drawer somewhere. From which she might occasionally extract it, if only for the purpose of drooling. She certainly couldn't see her way to chancing upon enough money to turn the project into reality, especially if the costs were non-subsidised, but who could tell what might happen in the future? There was always the Lottery. Should she ever decide to play it.

She was washing her plate and glass, with the radio playing quietly in the background, when the doorbell went.

He must have forgotten something, she thought irritably, because at a little before nine she was already beginning to wind down to her usual night-time routine of the news on television, followed by her book, followed by sleep. Or maybe he'd read the longing in her eyes at all his renovating proposals and in an act of pure sadism had written up all his plans in record time and intended to present her with them while she appeared vulnerable.

She smiled at the thought of that and was still smiling when she pulled open the front door and saw Max Forbes standing on her doorstep, still in his working clothes, although he'd removed his tie and undone the top button of his shirt. The breeze had ruffled his dark hair and the darkness outside made his face appear more angular than usual.

What was he doing here?

She had to resist the temptation to peer behind her towards the stairwell, to make sure that Chloe hadn't heard the ring of the doorbell and was drowsily making her way down the stairs.

A series of futile *whys* pounded in her head like the blows of a hammer. *Why* had she ever applied to the wretched company for a job? *Why* had she stupidly accepted the job with him when it had been offered? *Why* had she somehow found herself persuaded to stay on, even though her common sense had repeatedly lectured her on the foolhardiness of her actions? And, most searingly brutal of all, *why, why, why* had she yielded to him in every possible way? Made love with him? Fallen in love with him?

'Oh, hello,' she said. 'What are you doing here?' Her hair, curling down her back, was an unwelcome reminder of her femininity, as was the clinging short-sleeved top which she had flung on minutes before Andy Griggs had rang her doorbell, and the tight faded jeans.

'I was in the area and decided to come along and see how you had fared with Andy.' He leant against the door-frame, supporting himself with his arm, invading her space so that she stepped back a few inches, though not enough to give him any room to enter.

'You were in the area *again*? You seem to be in this area an awful lot.'

'Warwick is a small place.' He shrugged. 'Some friends live near here and asked me over for a drink. I think they want to make a match with their daughter. She's dull, rambling and conversationally unexciting. So, what did Andy say?'

'Well, he had a lot of good ideas.' Vicky gave in, though she still continued to block any possible sign of entry. 'I told him that I'd give the whole thing a great deal of thought and then get back to him.'

'But you won't commit yourself to anything because of what happened between us,' he prodded. 'One of the reasons I had to see you was to ask you something that's been on my mind for the past couple of hours. Do you feel unsafe when you're around me? If you do, then you might as well move on. Do you think that if we're alone together for more than five minutes I might grab you? Just because we happened to make love together once?'

'Of course not,' Vicky said tightly.

'Sure?' he asked softly, and she wondered whether he was trying to massage his own masculine ego by forcing her to admit that yes, he bothered her, and yes, she didn't think straight when she was around him.

'Quite sure. Now if that was all…'

'Actually, not quite all.' He produced some folded paper which he must have been holding the whole time but which she had failed to notice. 'This document you typed to Dobson is completely off track.'

'It is?' She reached out for it, embarrassed to have been picked up on an error, even though she had been particularly careful with this one because of the nature of the client.

'Have you got a PC with a printer? You'll have to make all the alterations on it now because I'm going to have to get back to the office and fax it off so that they have it sitting with them by five-thirty tomorrow morning when Bill's leaving for the Far East to consult with their sister firm over there about the operations.'

'Have you altered it on hard copy? If you have, you can leave it with me and I'll make sure it arrives on his desk by tomorrow morning.'

'Sorry.' He shook his head ruefully. 'I've added a couple of extra paragraphs, so we're going to have to go through this one together. Looks like I'm going to have to come in.'

CHAPTER SEVEN

MAX looked at the unwilling set of her face and the stiffness of her shoulders and managed to sustain his implacable smile with effort. He knew that he shouldn't be here at all, but that was a road he had no intention of going down. It led to too many frustrating questions.

'Is there a problem?' he asked politely, cocking his head to one side and shoving his hands deeper into his trouser pockets. 'I won't stay very long. Just long enough to get this damn thing done, and it goes without saying that I wouldn't have bothered coming here in the first place if you hadn't typed the wrong information in the first place.' He saw her colour deepen and felt a twinge of sheepish guilt. It galled him to realise that the changes he wanted to make were simply a handy excuse for showing up unannounced on her doorstep.

Somehow, somewhere, he couldn't get it out of his head that she was concealing a lover somewhere, and he vaguely thought that appearing out of the blue might smoke the man out.

'Well,' she hedged, looking up at him and chewing her bottom lip in a nervous gesture. 'I *was* about to go to bed...'

'At this hour?' He looked at his watch with overdone amazement. 'I've heard of quiet lives, but isn't nine o'clock taking things a little far?' He grinned, and wondered whether her intention of going to bed at an hour when most children over the age of thirteen were still up had anything to do with the mystery man, whose presence now seemed large, looming and gut-clenchingly real. Was he upstairs lying in the bed, sprawled and waiting? 'Don't tell me that you need your beauty sleep.' He tried to peer around her up the staircase, which was shrouded in darkness and she followed the line of his eyes with an irritated click of her tongue.

'Well, if you're quite sure that this won't take too long,' she told him, standing back to allow him access. Chloe was safely ensconced upstairs, sound asleep. There was almost no chance that she would suddenly awaken and come downstairs. Her sleeping habits had always been predictable. When she got into bed, she went to sleep, and only roused when the first fingers of light were beginning to worm their way past the closed curtains and into the bedroom. She wasn't one of those children who randomly prowled at odd hours in search of a warmer bed or a cup of juice or something to eat.

Nevertheless, she could feel her eyes anxiously flicker up the stairs as she led him away from all possible danger points and into the relative safety of the kitchen.

'I'm sorry about the mess,' she said perfunctorily, making a space on the kitchen table for him to spread the paperwork. The kitchen was small, but it was the brightest room in the house. No chance of subdued lighting creating any kind of atmosphere or playing havoc with her common sense. 'I've just finished eating.'

'Oh, really? What?' He made himself at home in one of the chairs, dumped the papers on the table and adjusted himself so that he could watch her as she self-consciously wiped the kitchen counter and put the kettle on to boil.

'Just some beans on toast.'

'I'm ravenous,' he told her casually. 'I dropped by the office on the way back from my meeting to collect this letter and then I came straight here to go through the corrections. Haven't had anything to eat since lunchtime.'

Vicky paused, turned to face him and met his candid gaze with a flicker of impatience. 'Are you hinting for something to eat?'

'Well, I *would* have had more than enough time to dine out this evening with…to have a meal if I hadn't been compelled to rush over here and get this matter sorted out post haste.'

'I'm afraid there's nothing fancy in the fridge.' She wondered what he would say if she offered him some fish fingers with potato shapes, or turkey dinosaurs with spaghetti hoops. 'I could fix you a cheese sandwich.'

'Beans on toast would be better.' He stretched out his long legs in front of him, crossing them at the ankles and clasped his hands behind his head. 'Haven't had that since…since I was a child, come to think of it.'

Vicky moved to the cupboard and began opening a can of baked beans, the contents of which she proceeded to dump into the saucepan which she'd used for heating her own only half an hour before. Then she stuck two slices of bread into the toaster and turned to face him, leaning against the counter, arms folded.

'What do your girlfriends cook for you?' she asked innocently, her eyes wide open. Girlfriends, she thought, as opposed to drunken one-night stands with employees. Girlfriends who did normal, girlfriendy things like cook meals instead of one-night stands who were in the position of being ordered to cancel their plans for the evening, prepare some food, and then, for that after-dinner treat, sit down and go through a load of work which would have to be typed until heaven only knew what time in the morning.

'Not beans on toast,' he said succinctly, and Vicky ploughed on with fatalistic intensity.

'What, then?'

'If I recall, a couple of them tried to prepare elaborate three-course meals...'

'Tried?'

'My kitchen isn't equipped for the preparation of elaborate three-course meals. God, that smells good. Any chance of some grated cheese over the top?'

The bread popped up and she liberally spread butter on it, then poured the entire tin of beans over both slices and finished the ensemble with a generous helping of grated cheese which melted into the beans. She stuck the plate in front of him and watched as he rearranged himself so that he could dig in. Anyone would think that he was enjoying a piece of the finest steak.

'If I recall, you have an extremely well-equipped kitchen.'

'Oh, that was before I had the new kitchen installed. Have you anything to drink? A cup of tea, perhaps? White, two sugars.'

'Sure that'll be all? I can always rustle up some plum crumble for afters,' Vicky informed him with sweetly biting sarcasm, unable to resist. He looked at her, fork poised *en route* to mouth, and she added quickly, 'It was a joke.'

'Plum crumble. A fading memory.'

'Oh, for goodness' sake! If your girlfriends can whip up gourmet meals, they're perfectly equipped to rustle up beans on toast and plum crumble. Please stop acting as though it requires talent.'

'A good plum crumble requires a great deal of talent,' he contradicted. 'And my *girlfriends* don't *rustle up* beans on toast for me, or *anything* else, for that matter, because I don't encourage that sort of thing.'

Vicky looked at him, mouth open, as though he had suddenly taken leave of his senses. 'You don't encourage that sort of thing?' she asked, confused. 'What's the point of having that kitchen if you never use it?' Comprehension dawned in her eyes. 'Oh, *I* get it. *You* are the one to do the cooking!' She imagined him whipping up an impressive array of food in under ten minutes and clad only in an apron. It was a sexist thought but irresistible. If *she* were the woman in his life, she would insist that he prepare her a meal, wearing nothing but a white apron, and she would fondle him as he cooked, distracting him with the tantalising flicker of her fingers on his body. She blinked away the sexy thought.

'Don't be absurd.' He finished eating with a gratified sigh of pleasure and stood up with the plate, heading to the sink and washing it without waiting for her to intercept him. 'I don't like women cooking for me, just in case it gives them ideas…'

'What kind of ideas?' Vicky asked, at a loss.

'Ideas of permanence.'

'Oh, *those* kind of ideas.' She nodded wisely. 'Very clever of you. What man in his right mind would want a woman to get ideas of permanence? When he can enjoy fruits of a relationship with no commitment or strings attached?'

Max turned very slowly to face her, and he slung the tea towel over his shoulder. Incongruously, it made him look all the more dangerously masculine. 'I don't think this has much to do with the purpose of my visit, do you?' he asked softly, and Vicky felt herself flush with shame. She'd reluctantly let him come in through lack of choice, even though she realised the necessity of getting him out as quickly as possible, and yet here she was, indulging in pointless conversation just because her curiosity was niggling away at her.

'Right.' She briskly wiped her hands on a towel, sat down at the kitchen table and shuffled the papers around to face her. The first set of corrections, which were done insultingly in bright red pen, made her frown. 'Are you *sure* these haven't been typed correctly? I mean you're just rephrasing what was said in the original draft.'

'I've added bits in,' Max informed her testily.

'Relevant bits?'

'Are you questioning me?'

'No, of course not, I just wondered...' Her voice trailed off into silence as she quickly inspected the rest of the documents. With a spot of rapid typing, she would be able to get this lot done in under forty-five minutes. 'My computer's in the utility,' she said, standing up and flicking through the paper. 'Give me a few minutes and I should be able to have this all typed up for you.' When he stood up, she eyed him sceptically. 'I shouldn't bother,' she said, 'The utility's a bit on the cramped side.'

'Why do you store your PC in your utility?' He ignored her request to stay put, and followed her through the kitchen door, briefly out into the cold, and then into a separate shed which housed a washing machine, a tumble drier, various clothes lines which were coiled in disarray on the floor, a sink and a stack of wellingtons shoved in the corner. Vicky switched on an electric heater, pulled a chair in front of the beaten-up desk on which the computer sat, beady-eyed and waiting.

'I keep meaning to move it,' Vicky admitted, switching on and watching the flat black screen jump into life. 'When I got back from Australia, this was the first thing I bought, thinking that I could work from home if need be, and I wasn't home when it came, so my neighbour got them to stick it in here and the thought of moving the whole lot out and into one of the bedrooms was so exhausting that—' She peered at the screen, licked her lips and clicked to open a new file and rapidly began to type '—I left it here. Besides, I like it in here.'

'You *like* your utility?'

'There's no need to sound so surprised,' she said tartly, glancing up from her typing to glare at him briefly. 'Everyone has a special place. *You* must have a special place. Haven't you?'

'No,' he said bluntly. 'If you discount my bed.'

'Well, *this* is my special place,' Vicky informed him, looking at the screen. 'I used to have picnics here when I was a kid. Made it kind of exciting because it wasn't attached to the house and Mum and Dad didn't mind me using it in winter because they could stick the heater in and warm it up. And whenever Mum did the ironing in here, I made sure that one of my picnics was in operation.' Vicky smiled at the sudden memory. 'She spent half her time tripping over my dolls.'

'Happy childhood stuff, that.' She hadn't realised but he'd moved directly over her, and he now leaned down, encircling her with his arms so that his head was on a level with hers, and he could read the document as she typed it. She could feel his warm breath against her neck and her thought processes thickened in response. Her breasts were beginning to ache. Would he see her nipples hardening behind the fine, stretchy cotton of the T-shirt? She wanted to glance down and evaluate what her wretched body was doing, but didn't dare.

Instead she frowned in concentration at what she was doing and tried to work even faster. On either side of her chair, his arms were like two steel bands, trapping her in. If she moved five inches in either direction, flesh would meet flesh. The thought sent another wave of light-headed giddiness racing through her.

'No, no. Those figures don't look quite right. Go back to the last page.' When she did, he reached out and traced the offending lines on the computer screen, his arm way too close to her for comfort, but shifting her body would only put her into contact with his other arm. Vicky tried to look knowledgeable, but in fact she barely heard when he instructed her to carry on. She just knew that reaching the last page couldn't come too soon.

When she was finished, she saved the lot and then asked him whether he would mind switching on the printer. He moved away and she felt her body go limp before she straightened up and began printing.

'Well done,' he said, as page after page was printed and he collected the lot, standing to one side with his hip resting gently against the washing machine, pushing his fingers through his dark hair as he narrowly inspected what she'd just written. If he made the mistake of telling her that there were one or two things still to correct, she felt she might fling the computer at his handsome head. It wasn't fair that he could waltz into her private life like this and shake the hell out of it. She needed all the personal space she could find to come to terms with what he had done to her, and showing up on her doorstep unannounced wasn't helping matters along.

'Is everything in order?' Vicky asked, vacating the chair rather than face the possibility of another trapped situation. She waited, and when he finally nodded switched off the computer terminal and then, for the sake of safety, pulled out the plugs. 'Just in case,' she informed him, when she realised that he was watching her with an odd expression. 'It's an old house.'

'Which brings me to Andy. What did he have to say?'

He slipped the papers into the thin leather case and followed her out of the utility and back through the kitchen door, which Vicky locked behind them.

'Just that work needs to be done on the place. There's some damp.' She reflected that the tone of voice used by the architect when he had said this implied *rampant* damp rather than just the odd patch here and there. 'He's going to send a report through with all his suggestions and costings in a few days' time and—' she shrugged, folding her arms '—I'll have a look at it.' She looked at him, refusing to invite further debate on the subject. Things had gone quite smoothly, considering. She'd managed to school her features into a professional, unflappable mask and, more to the point, her daughter had remained obediently asleep upstairs, but it was best not to tempt fate. She had a nasty habit of kicking you in the teeth when you did that.

'I take it that you don't feel the inclination to expand on that,' he said, turning to face her with the leather case tucked under one arm.

'It's late.'

'It's—' he looked pointedly and for an aggravatingly long time at his watch '—a little after nine-thirty.'

'That's what I mean. It's late.'

'I can't believe you consider nine-thirty *late*.'

Vicky shuffled on her feet and gave up the attempt to outstare him. 'I've never been a night bird,' she mumbled vaguely, and he, even more aggravatingly, raised his eyebrows in amused cynicism at this non response.

'Would you say that it's too late for a nightcap?' he asked, adding smoothly, 'Of coffee? I wasn't implying a stiff drink.' His eyes caught hers and she could see the follow-up to that mirrored in the peculiar grey eyes. *We both know where alcohol can take us.* Or, at least, she was certain that that was what she read there before he lowered his eyes.

'A quick cup.' she fought against irritation. Her personal involvement with him, her feelings for him, were not appropriate, and she would have to fight against allowing that to seep out into her voice. It occurred to her that she could take the craven way out of the whole situation and put him in a position where he would have no alternative but to sack her. Gross impertinence, whatever that comprised, would do the trick, she was sure, but she quailed at the idea. Aside from anything else, it would not do to have a poor reference from him. He was an important person in the area, as she was finding out on a daily basis, and she knew that, if he wanted, he could easily scupper her chances of landing a good job locally.

'Of course. I wouldn't dream of keeping you from your nightly routine,' he murmured politely.

'I didn't say that my *nightly routine* involved going to bed at nine. I do *get out*, you know.' She turned on the tap to fill the kettle with a ferocity that had the water splashing out at her.

'Oh, do you? Where? Are there many night spots around here? I must say, I tend to head back to London for night life.'

'Depends on what kind of night life you're looking for.' She hoped she sounded calm and mysterious and in possession of a night life, instead of evasive because a night life was something she had given up on a long time ago. Even when she'd lived in Australia fear of reprisal from Shaun had altered her social habits, so that, in the end, she had tended to stay put with her daughter, inviting the occasional girlfriend over to her aunt's house for supper, but avoiding anything that indicated fun.

Fun, she'd been told, was not to be on her agenda.

Shaun had not wanted her, but the thought that someone else might had driven him into a frenzy. He'd liked controlling her life, dropping in when it suited him, watching her with sadistic amusement as she scurried nervously around, fully aware that one wrong word might just be enough to threaten the quality of her life. Looking back at it, she was amazed that she'd allowed herself to live for so long in the grip of perpetual fear, but at the time she'd really imagined that there was no way out. She'd never questioned that he would take Chloe away from her if she didn't do as he said. She'd witnessed his rages and his unpredictable behaviour and she'd always known that he was more than capable of it. Now, she could reason that the law would have stopped him, but back then the law had played second fiddle to fear.

'I suppose so.' He reached out for the mug of coffee and their fingers briefly brushed. 'What kind of night life would *you* be looking for? You're a young girl. Still clubbing?'

'Oh good grief. I haven't been clubbing since…since for ever.' She almost smiled at the thought of going to a night club with a young daughter in tow.

'Why not?'

'Because…I don't enjoy that sort of thing,' she said vaguely, which anyway was the truth.

'So you…?'

'Go to the movies, all the usual stuff. Drink your coffee or it'll go cold.' By way of example, she swallowed some large mouthfuls of hers and laid the mug on the counter with finality. She was exasperated to see that he refused to take the hint, sipping at his as though he had all the time in the world to kill.

'You're distracting me, standing there tapping one foot and fiddling with your fingers.'

Vicky, who hadn't realised that she was doing either of those things, promptly stopped both. Annoyingly, her mind seized on the word *distracted* and she wondered what he'd meant. Did he mean that he couldn't take his eyes off her? Hardly, she thought with a trace of wry realism. Shaun had been fond of reminding her that, were it not for the striking colour of her hair, she would have faded into the background; she lacked spark.

He drained his cup, stood up and headed out of the kitchen with an abruptness that had her scurrying off behind him after a few seconds of disorientation.

'Right. Thanks for your help, Vicky,' he told her in a clipped voice. 'Grudging though it was.'

'I'm sorry. I didn't mean to appear grudging.' Even when she said that, she knew that she *sounded* grudging. 'It's just that I'm one of those boring creatures of routine, and having my routine put out of joint makes me go into a funny mood.'

'I'll remember that for the future,' he said drily. He pulled open the front door and at that split instant two things happened.

A sharp gust of wind blew into the hall, lifting her hair and then rushing past her to the kitchen door, which had been left open.

The slam of the kitchen door reverberated in the house like the sudden, startling clap of thunder, and there was an answering cry from up the stairs.

Vicky's blood froze in her veins. For a second or two she truly thought that she might have been turned to ice, then she was galvanised into action. It was as though her brain, temporarily disabled, had suddenly shot into overdrive and in the space of a few seconds had processed all the horrific possibilities that could arise for the sound of that childish voice crying out from a bedroom upstairs.

'What the...?' He stepped back into the hall and she placed the palms of her hands flat on his chest in a vain attempt to prevent him coming in any further. 'What's going on here?' he said sharply, his eyes narrowing on the empty staircase.

As if on cue, Chloe yelled, 'Mummy! Where are you?'

Vicky turned on her feet and raced up the stairs, taking them two at a time, her heart beating like a steam-engine in her chest. She was out of breath by the time she made it up to the bedroom. She shot in, shutting the door behind her, because she was pretty sure that Max would now be back in the house, waiting for her to return and offer some explanation, if not heading up the staircase in a mission to find out what was going on.

'Shh!' she hissed, edging over to the bed where her daughter was sitting up, bolt upright, yawning and rubbing her eyes. 'The wind blew the kitchen door shut, honey.'

'Oh. I thought it was thunder.'

'You need to go back to sleep. Tomorrow's school.' She stroked the forehead and plastered a soothing smile on her face. It made her feel one-dimensional. 'And you know Mrs Edwards doesn't like sleepyheads in her class!' If she sounded any more hearty, she thought, she would end up alarming her daughter instead of reassuring her. She held the little face between her hands.

'Can I come downstairs for something to drink?'

'No, honey.'

'Why not?'

'Because there's nothing in the fridge. Must go to the supermarket tomorrow.'

'Can I check for myself?'

'Too dark, Clo.'

'Pleeeaaaasssssseeee...?'

Instead of uttering a few calm words that would send

her drowsy daughter back off to the Land of Nod, it appeared, Vicky thought, that she had succeeded in rousing her completely. In a minute Chloe would be out of the bed and ready for fun and games.

'Tell you what,' Vicky said, 'I'll go and have a look and bring you up a milk shake. I might just be able to rummage up some milk, I think.'

'When?'

'In a minute.'

That explanation seemed to do the trick, because Chloe subsided in a satisfied heap back onto the bed and within minutes her eyes were closed and her breathing was regular.

Very quietly, Vicky tiptoed out of the bedroom, closing the door gently behind her, then she flew down the stairs, half hoping that Max would have somehow left the house, ignoring his understandable curiosity, respecting her need for privacy. Her hopes, such as they were, were dashed by the sight of him looming darkly in the hallway, front door ominously closed, a grim expression on his face.

'Care to tell me what's going on?'

'I'd rather not, actually,' Vicky said, holding herself erect and willing herself to feel angrily invaded instead of guilty and terrified. Max Forbes would be able to sniff out the scent of guilt and terror and as soon as he did that he would be on her case like a ton of bricks. She decided that giving him some of the truth might be the best idea. 'Or rather, not at this moment. Please.'

'Because it's way past your bedtime?' His mouth twisted cynically and she flinched from the brutal disbelief in his eyes. 'And of course, you weren't lying, were you? You *do* go to bed early because that's what having a child does to a woman, isn't it? Screws up her sleeping habits? How old is he? Five, six, seven, older?'

'It's a she, not a he,' Vicky said wearily. 'And I'll explain it all to you tomorrow, if you'll just go away now.'

'Not,' he said coldly, 'on your life. You lied about her at your interview and as your employer I have every right to know what other lies you've told.'

'I haven't told any other lies,' Vicky said uncomfortably.

'I think *I'll* be the judge of that.' He took a few steps further into the hall and Vicky couldn't resist it. She glanced towards the staircase, which was thankfully empty, then she turned to face him, her hands balled into tight fists, her mouth set in a stubborn line.

'All right,' she muttered through clenched teeth, 'I'll tell you what you want to know. In the sitting room. And then when I've finished I want you to leave. Is that clear?'

He ignored the command in her voice, as she had known he would, but at least he followed her into the sitting room. Somehow, pouring out her personal life, highly edited though the version would be, in a cold, dark hallway, was not what Vicky wanted.

He sprawled on the chair, filling it out in a way that made it seem diminutive and inadequate, and Vicky quietly closed the door behind her. Then she perched on the arm of the chair facing him, her fingers laced together on her knees, her mind whirling with the frantic need to get rid of him as soon as possible. All her initial fears, which had somehow been sidelined over the past few weeks, rose up and threatened to engulf her. In a stroke, he could bring her life crashing down around her ears. He could take Chloe away from her if he ever discovered the child's identity. He could certainly ensure that her working life in the area was ended. He was a man of influence and power, and that could speak in tongues she couldn't even begin to understand. She forced herself to think rationally. He had no idea that Chloe was his niece and there was no reason why he should ever find out.

For a split instant, she felt a twinge of guilt that she was wilfully depriving her daughter of a blood relative, but then the instinct for survival took over and she drew a deep breath.

'Okay. I have a child. She's five years old and I know that I should have told you about her, but I was scared.'

'Scared of *what*?' The curl of his lips informed her that he was not prepared to be sympathetic.

'You have no idea what it's like…'

'No? Then why don't you enlighten me?'

The expression on his face made her feel like a whingeing damsel in a Victorian melodrama. 'It's very hard being a single-parent family,' Vicky said quietly. 'It's fine for you to sit there and offer comments about the situation, but you have no idea how difficult it is being on your own with a child.'

'Where's the father?'

'He's dead. He died in a car crash.'

'Australian, was he?'

'He lived there, yes. I lied about my daughter because I felt that having a child would be held against me when it came to getting a job. Most employers shy away the minute they hear that there's a young child on the scene. They foresee lots of broken appointments and late arrivals and days off. I was going to tell you, but I suppose I just kept putting it off because I knew you'd react the way you did.' She sighed. 'You're right and I was wrong. I should never have taken the job with you in the first place.' That much, at any rate, was heartfelt.

'I can't believe that you resorted to all this subterfuge to conceal the fact that you have a child. It doesn't make any sense.' He frowned and stared at her narrowly until she looked away. 'I can understand the patterns now,' he mused slowly, 'the need to leave work on the dot, the evasiveness when it came to working late or overtime. All that slots into place. What *I'm* having a problem with is the *why*. *Why* lie in the first place? The majority of women working for me are married, with kids. We're not talking about an old-fashioned, chauvinistic, medieval establishment here. We're not talking about the sort of place where gossips would ferret out an unmarried mother and send her to the gallows for punishment.' He gave a dry, hard laugh. 'So why don't you tell me the full story? *What else is there?*'

'There's nothing else,' Vicky said, standing up. 'If you feel that you can't work with me now, then I'll understand.' She brushed a few non-existent specks of dust off her jeans and then edged behind her chair, gripping the back of it with her hands. Why did he think that she was still hiding something? Could he read what was going on in her mind from the expression on her face? Did he have X-ray eyes? She felt as though her nervous system had been put through a shredder.

'And there's another thing,' he said pensively, stroking his chin with one long finger and making no attempt to budge.

'What? What's another thing?' She could barely conceal the jumpiness in her voice, even though she knew that the more jumpy she sounded, the more penetrating would be his scrutiny of what she had told him.

'The myriad times you mention that you *might just leave the company*. Why do you do that, I wonder?'

Vicky, for her part, wondered desperately why he didn't leave her house. All that musing and speculation was making the hairs on the back of her neck stand on end.

'Are you one of these women who needs constant re-assurances?'

'*One of these women who needs constant reassurances?* Oh, please!'

'Then why are you always threatening to walk out? There's no need to feel insecure. You've told me your dark little secret—' he allowed a few nasty seconds to elapse, just to remind her that he was quite aware of the holes in her storyline '—and I don't think your status will affect your job.' He stood up and she very nearly groaned with relief. 'So I expect to see you in the morning,' he added, walking towards the sitting room door and resting his hand lightly on the door handle, 'and you needn't worry,' he said seriously, 'that I'll make any unreasonable demands on you. I'm not an ogre. I do appreciate that working women with children cannot be as accommodating as single, child-free women. But—' his eyes narrowed on her '—I would have appreciated the truth from the beginning, and what I *don't* expect is to discover that any more lies have been told. Got it? You're in a job that sometimes requires the utmost confidentiality. A loose-tongued liar is the last person I need working for me.'

'I'm not a loose-tongued liar! I made *one* mistake, told *one* lie, for which I apologise. I don't make a habit of running around lying to anyone and everyone. But if you feel that way, then I'm more than happy to quit!' She looked at him with mutinous determination and he appeared to think the matter over.

'One chance, Vicky, because you're so damn good at what you do. But that's it.'

Vicky murmured something fairly inaudible. She had just lived through the most harrowing couple of hours since she had returned to England. Her vocal cords were apparently giving up through sheer stress.

He abandoned his condemnation of her and assumed a
lighter tone. 'I can understand why the thought of reno-
vations to this house hold so much appeal. I expect you've
been thinking along the lines of playrooms and places to
store toys?'

He fully opened the door, and Vicky saw Chloe before
Max, who was still looking at her. She was standing at the
bottom of the staircase, nicely caught in a pool of light,
her dark hair tousled from sleeping, her right hand clutching the moth-eaten teddy that had been her faithful com-
panion since birth.

Max, following the startled widening of her eyes, turned
around, and whatever he had been saying died on his lips.

'You promised to bring me up a milk shake, Mum,'
Chloe said. 'I'm thirsty.'

CHAPTER EIGHT

THERE was a sense of doomed inevitability about the whole thing. In the space of a second or two, Vicky accepted that fate had just been playing games with her ever since she had accepted the job, waiting for this very moment to evolve so that she could have the last laugh.

She watched the scenario unfolding in front of her and realised that there was nothing more that she could do.

Chloe, who had barely noticed the presence of another adult in the room, now became aware of Max standing to one side, stepping out of the shadows, and her eyes opened wide in shock and puzzlement.

'Shaun?' she whispered uncertainly. She scuttled over to Vicky, her eyes fixed on Max, and clutched the proffered hand. Vicky reached down and swept her daughter into her arms, wrapping her protectively into her, with one hand cupping the back of Chloe's dark head. She knew that her hands were trembling. 'Mummy, what's Shaun doing here?'

'It's not Shaun,' Vicky whispered, aware that Max's eyes were boring into her, demanding answers. 'How about that milk shake?'

'She called me *Shaun*.' Max regained his power of speech, but before he could launch into a series of questions Vicky looked at him sharply and held up one finger for him to keep quiet, then she walked away towards the kitchen, still hanging on to Chloe, although she was now aware that her daughter's head had popped up and was doubtless surveying the unnerving vision in front of her with childish curiosity and apprehension.

Disconcertingly, Max had followed in her wake. Vicky had a vision of them both avidly looking at one another, and the weight of all the explanations lurking in the not-too-distant future made her feel sick and weary. She switched on the kitchen light and, still not looking at Max, she sat Chloe on the kitchen counter and proceeded to pour milk into a glass, add some chocolate powder and stir, really as though everything was fine and her life hadn't been suddenly turned on its head. It was the calm before the storm. She felt like breaking into hysterical laughter and had to fight the urge, because calm was what was needed. A calm hand, a steady head and a cool determination.

'Okay, honey,' she whispered unsteadily to her daughter, whose attention she now had to fight to retrieve. 'You can have your milk shake in bed and Mummy will explain everything to you in the morning.'

'Has Shaun come back from Heaven to visit us?'

'No, darling. Of course not. This man here just *looks* like him, that's all.' *Heaven? Shaun Forbes?* She walked past Max and proceeded up the stairs with her daughter. 'There's no need to follow us,' she addressed the figure behind her in a cold voice. 'I *will* come back down.'

'You'd better.'

Don't you dare threaten me, she wanted to say, but fear made her keep quiet, relieved at least that he'd turned and was heading back down.

'But who *is* he?' Chloe asked unsteadily, as she was deposited onto the bed and handed her glass of milk shake. 'Why does he look like Shaun?' She drank a mouthful of milk shake and watched her mother over the rim of the glass. Vicky tried to imagine what must be going through her daughter's head. Surprise, bewilderment, all muddled up because she was still sleepy. Certainly no excitement. Her father had made no effort to try and cultivate a relationship with her and, consequently, Chloe had seen him as virtually a stranger, one who brought her the occasional present, depending on his mood and whether any money happened to be available at the time. From the very beginning he'd insisted on being called Shaun by her which, as it turned out, couldn't have been better, because *daddy* implied an affectionate intimacy which was patently lacking in their relationship. Later on, indifference had given way to a certain amount of wariness, because she'd been able to see the effect he had on her mother, even though Vicky had done her utmost to protect her daughter from her father's nastier sides.

'They're related,' Vicky said, smoothing the dark hair with her hand. She kept her voice as low, as soporific and as expressionless as possible, and she kept up the stroking until Chloe's eyes began to flicker shut, then she carefully removed the glass of milk shake and placed it very quietly on the bedside table. 'I'll talk to you about it in the morning.' Right now, *morning* seemed a long way away. In fact most things, including normality, seemed a long way away, with Max Forbes prowling around downstairs, waiting for her to reappear so that he could start firing questions at her. The questions, she thought sickly, making a hushed departure from her daughter's room and gently closing the door behind her, weren't as terrifying as the prospect of what would come swiftly in their wake. Therein lay a whole murky morass of possible avenues, none of which she cared to contemplate.

At the top of the stairs she paused, took a deep breath and then headed down the stairs and into the sitting room, where Max was waiting for her, as she knew he would be, lounging by the window with his hands stuck into his pockets. He waited in perfect silence as she sidled across to the nearest chair and sat down. Waited and watched until she could feel her body perspiring and her nerves stretching tighter and tighter, pulling her to breaking point.

He was waiting for her to start babbling, she thought. He probably figured that she would babble herself right into a corner, from which he could then proceed to bar her exit and do precisely as he pleased.

She cracked, though managed to hang on to a fairly steady voice. 'I suppose you want an explanation of what just went on.' When he didn't say anything, she carried on with rising anger, 'Well, standing there in silence isn't going to get either of us anywhere!'

Instead of responding with a verbal outburst, he strode towards the door and closed it, then he strolled towards her, so that she was reluctantly forced to stare up at him. She winced when her eyes met his. Judging from the expression on his face, whatever deductions he had reached showed that he was halfway there to providing his own correct explanation.

'The door's shut,' he said silkily, 'and you can consider yourself trapped here until you tell me what's going on. And don't even think about skirting over the details. I want you to start at the beginning, leaving nothing out, and then—' he moved across to the sofa, sat down, crossed one ankle over his thigh and looked at her '—I shall decide what to do with you.'

'*What to do with me?* You can't do anything with me!' She sounded a lot braver than she felt and her fingers were twining together nervously.

'Of course I can.' He shot her a patient, rueful look that didn't disguise the cold, hard, reptilian determination in his eyes. 'But we won't go into any of that just yet.'

Vicky felt a quiver of dread race along her spine. She cleared her throat, but when she opened her mouth to speak she could barely enunciate what she wanted to say.

'Start at the beginning,' he told her in the same kind voice that was designed to turn her into a nervous wreck. 'Which—' he leaned forward and surveyed her musingly, his head tilted to one side '—I take it involved my brother, Shaun? That was the name your daughter uttered, wasn't it? *Shaun?* With that look of stunned recognition in her eyes?' The veneer of kindness was disappearing, as she had known it would sooner or later. '*Not,*' he added softly, 'that I wouldn't have guessed her identity. She could be my brother's clone. Same hair, same colouring, same eyes... Little secrets *do* have a way of slipping out sooner or later, don't they?' He bared his teeth in a smile while she continued to look at him with mesmerised apprehension. 'Or perhaps,' he continued languidly, 'slipping out is a bit of a misnomer...because that would imply a mistake, wouldn't it? When there must be a name for the deliberate exposure of a so-called secret...wouldn't you say? What word would I be searching for here, do you think?' He stood up and strolled towards the window, idly flicking back the curtain and peering outside for a few seconds before reverting back to his inspection of her face. His movements were lazy and unhurried. Here was a man, she thought, with all the time in the world to pin her to the wall and crucify her. She swallowed hard.

'What are you talking about?' she mumbled.

'Tut, tut, tut. Please. No games.' Another threatening baring of the teeth, then he sat back down. 'Just the truth. When did you decide to hunt me down so that you could— hey, presto—turn over your trump card and take me for every penny I've got?'

'Hunt you down?' Vicky shook her head in utter confusion. 'Fleece you? *What* are you talking about?'

'Stop it! Now!' He sat forward and punched one clenched fist into the palm of his hand with such force that she jumped. 'What happened? Did you meet my brother out in Australia and decide that he was a good match? A good match, that is, until you discovered that his outgoings usually exceeded his incomings by several thousands per month? Or maybe even when you found that out you still decided that there was enough there to make it worthwhile, but only a child could have got the commitment... Is that when you decided to become pregnant? Backfired, though, didn't it...because he didn't marry you, did he?'

'You've got this all wrong.' Her mind tried to grapple with all the misconceptions being hurled at her but it was lagging behind. As fast as he tossed one accusation at her, and before she'd had time to deal with it, he was moving on to something else, some other nightmarish misunderstanding. From one correct assumption, he'd woven his own theories, and was now in the process of shooting her down with them.

'No,' she began a little more forcefully, 'that's not what happened at all...'

'I gather. But things must really have looked grim when Shaun died. No wedlock, no cash... What was there for a poor girl to do but hot-foot it over here to England and check out what further sources of finance were available?'

'Look, this has gone far enough!' She stood up, trembling, but her legs were unsteady and she slumped back onto the chair.

'I don't think so. Actually, I don't think we've even begun as yet.' There was grim resolution stamped on his face. Not in a million years would anyone have ever guessed that the man sitting opposite her possessed anything resembling a sense of humour. That he had made her giggle, made her blush, had touched her and turned her body to fire. Now the opposite was happening. With every word, her body was turning to ice.

'You played it cool, though. I have to admit it. My hat's off to you, and I'm as sceptical as they go when it comes to a gold-digger.'

'I am not a *gold*-digger!' She spat the words out. With anger and frustration she watched his dark eyebrows raise in incredulous disbelief.

'No? So are you telling me that it was sheer coincidence that you managed to wangle a job working for your ex-lover's brother?'

'I didn't *wangle* a job,' Vicky muttered miserably. 'I just—'

'Just what? Happened to be walking past a company that carried the Forbes name? And decided to apply for a job? Without it ever occurring to you that the similarity of the names might indicate something?'

'You don't understand. I saw the name and yes, I was curious...'

'And a little curiosity got your brain churning, didn't it? You must have thought you'd hit jackpot when you saw me! Now all you had to do was reel me in, slowly but surely, and you took your time. No rushing in and producing the child like a magician pulling a rabbit out of a hat...'

'*Chloe. The child's* name is *Chloe.*' His phraseology sparked off a memory that bit into her like acid. Shaun had called his daughter *the child*. It had enraged her then, and just hearing the same, dehumanising words come from his brother's mouth enraged her now. 'And, for your information,' she said vehemently, standing up and discovering that her wobbly legs could actually support her now, 'the thought of getting money from your brother or any other member of his wretched family was the last thing on my mind!' She walked over to where he was sitting and loomed over him like an angry, red-haired, avenging angel.

'And you expect me to believe that?' His lips twisted into a sneer of disbelief and, without pausing to think, she raised her hand and slapped him hard on the face, hard enough for his head to swing back and for her hand to feel as though every bone in it had been broken. The display of violence surprised her as much as it surprised him but, before she could step back, his hand had shot out, grasping hers by the wrist and yanking her forward so that she had to catch herself from toppling on top of him.

'You knew exactly what you were doing. Why don't you admit it? Why else did you accept the job offer unless to ingratiate yourself with me, until an opportune moment came for you to reveal your little secret? Damn you!' His grey eyes were blazingly furious and Vicky shrank back with a small cry of dismay and fright. For the first time it really hit home that his armoury of weapons, should he choose to deploy them, was extensive.

As if reading her mind, he gave her hand another fierce jerk and then said in a dangerously soft voice, 'Well, my dear, I'm a completely different kettle of fish to my brother. When you decided to play with me, you decided to play with fire—and fire burns. Do you understand what I could do to you? I could drag you through the courts and demand partial custody of the...of my...my brother's child. In fact, I could probably swing to take her away from you. After all, money talks, and she would be in line for a very large fortune.'

Vicky felt the colour drain from her face. 'You c-couldn't,' she stammered. 'You wouldn't...'

He looked at her for a few seconds, holding her terrified

gaze, then he released her hand as though touching it was distasteful. Vicky took a few steps back, her eyes still clamped on his face, searching to discover whether he had meant what he'd said. *Surely not?* The law wouldn't hand over custody of her child to this man, anyway, although the money element was enough to keep a seed of doubt planted in some corner of her mind.

'Why not?' he shrugged, then rubbed the side of his face again, where she had hit him. She sincerely hoped that she'd broken a few of his teeth in the process, but if she had he was successfully hiding the fact.

'What do you mean, *why not*?' Vicky asked in an appalled whisper. 'Chloe's the beginning, the middle and the end of my whole life! If you try and take her away...' Her voice began to waver and, without warning, she broke down. No warm-up of sniffles, no watery eyes as a prelude—she just collapsed into tears, loud, distraught, uncontrollable sobbing that was imbued with all the grief that she'd experienced over the past few years, starting with her mother's death.

'Oh, for God's sake,' Max muttered, standing up, 'I don't intend to take your child away from you. It was a threat.' He thrust a handkerchief into her hand and Vicky clutched it gratefully, pressing it to her eyes. 'How the hell do you think I feel?' he all but yelled, striding restlessly around the room, his fingers raking through his dark hair. With her face pressed against the handkerchief and her head downturned, she could still feel the energy emanating out of him like an electric current.

'One minute I have a good secretary, the next minute I discover that the good secretary is the mother of my niece! And you stand there, sobbing and pleading with me to believe that there was no hint of a hidden agenda anywhere on the dinner menu?'

Vicky lifted puffy, red eyes to him and said, 'Yes.'

'*Yes? Yes?* Is that *all* you have to say on the matter?
You just *expect* me to take you at your word and write it
all off to *quirky coincidence*?' He paused in front of her.
His dark hair was a mess and his searching eyes made her
look away hurriedly.

'Yes,' she repeated weakly. 'I mean, that's what *I've*
written it all off to.' She sighed deeply and then proceeded
to do origami with the handkerchief, folding it and unfolding it until he finally snatched it off her and shoved it
back into his pocket.

'Sit down,' he commanded, 'and explain.'

'Only if you're prepared to listen to me.'

'I'll try.'

It was better than nothing, even though his expression,
while not seething with hostility as it had been a couple
of minutes ago, was still cynical enough to make her want
to abandon her explanations before she'd even begun.

'I met your brother in Australia when I was nineteen.
I...' She stumbled in the face of the uphill task facing her.
How could she summarise six years of her life in the space
of fifteen minutes when every day of every month of all
those years was filled with emotional detail? She took a
deep breath. 'I'd gone to Australia to live with my aunt—
well, you know all of this, but when my mother died, I
just couldn't face staying on in England. My mum and I
had always planned to go on a joint holiday to visit Aunt
Ruth and, well, it seemed as though the moment had come
when Mum was no longer around. I couldn't bear being
in the house but I couldn't bear the thought of selling it,
either. That's why I rented it out. Mum's funeral was on
the Tuesday and by the following Tuesday I was on a
plane leaving England for what I thought would be six
months. I ended up staying for nearly six years.'

'And why was that?' The timbre of his deep voice almost made her start.

'Lots of reasons.' She shrugged and avoided his silver eyes. 'The weather was good. Aunt Ruth was so thrilled to see me that she managed to persuade me to apply for an extension on my visa and then, when that came through, it seemed as though destiny wanted me to stay. And then I landed the job working as a personal assistant to the director of a public relations company. It was a huge responsibility and I adored it, even though I knew that James mainly hired me because of my English accent. He missed England. He used to say that having me around was like having his own private rose garden in the office.' Her lips softened into a smile of fond memory and Max scowled. He could feel his fingers pushing against the fabric of the chair from the effort of controlling his rampant rage and jealousy. Knowing that his brother had slept with her, fathered a child by her, fuelled a sense of obliterating anger. He wanted to shout and rip the house down. He could barely breathe properly, and here she was, smiling at the mention of her ex-boss. Another lover, perhaps? One more trophy? He struggled to maintain some balance, although his jaws ached.

'How nice,' he said tightly. 'And was he another one of your lovers, alongside my brother?'

'That's a horrible thing to say!'

'Is it?' He could feel himself wanting to hurt her and steeled himself against the temptation. 'I took you at face value and now here I am, confronted by a woman who had a child by my brother, slept with me and has God knows how many more skeletons locked away in her closet somewhere.'

'There *are* no more skeletons. I know you think...you feel—'

'*Think* what? *Feel* what?'

'Angry with me. Disappointed...'

Max tried to modulate the decibel level of his voice when he next spoke. It wouldn't do to have the neighbours flying over to the house because of the noise. '*Angry? Disappointed?* Yes, those two will do for starters.'

Vicky looked uncertainly at him, scared at the underlying savagery she sensed and, worse, understood. She knew that she'd done far more than disappoint him. She knew that she'd destroyed his trust for ever and the thought of that made her feel sick.

'I met your brother while I was working for James.' She leaned back into the chair and closed her eyes. 'And I'll admit that for a while, I was...I suppose, infatuated with him. I had just gone through a very bad patch, I was still trying to recover from Mum's death and Shaun was like a tonic. Always on a high. Happy. I was completely taken in with his live-for-today attitude. It was just what I needed.' She risked a look at Max from under her lashes. He was sitting very still. Only the muscle in his jaw showed that he was hearing a word she said.

'We started dating and it was fun, for a while. I'd never experienced life in the fast lane, and Shaun was very much someone who lived in the fast lane. Sports cars, late-night parties, exotic friends. It was all very exciting for a while.'

Her words were drifting in and out of his head. The *for a while* lifted his spirits temporarily, because it promised that worse was to come, but he found that he couldn't focus on anything she was saying. Not really. He was too busy thinking about her in bed with Shaun, too busy feeling betrayed by her casual deception, too busy agonising over the fact that nothing she could say or do, however horrendous, could kill his fast-growing feelings towards her.

'What was that?'

'I asked what…what *you* thought of your brother,' Vicky said timidly. She had sometimes wondered whether she hadn't misjudged Shaun, or whether there hadn't been something in *her* that had driven him to turn into a monster when he found himself in her company. Maybe it hadn't been *him* at all. Maybe the fault had lain with *her*.

'Wild. Reckless. Prone to excess. I'm surprised you found him so appealing. Did you enjoy living on a knife's edge?'

'I suppose I must have. For a while.'

'You keep saying that. *For a while* this, *for a while* that. What does that *mean*?' He shot her a brooding, glowering look and then abruptly stood up and resumed his restless pacing around the room, as though the confines of the chair were stifling him.

'It *means* that after a few months I…I began to see another side to your brother. A much…darker side.'

Max stopped pacing and turned to look at her. 'What *darker side*?'

'Did you communicate with Shaun?'

'Oh, yes. Christmas cards.' His mouth twisted bitterly. 'My attempts to communicate with my brother ended when we were about…sixteen. From there on in we might just as well have been strangers.'

'Then perhaps you don't know that Shaun—'

'Dabbled with drugs?' he asked intuitively, watching the contours of her expressive face. 'Of course I knew. It was one of the reasons he was sent to Australia. His opportunity to wipe the slate clean and start over. I tried to talk some sense into him before he went, tried to make him see that he was damaging himself by taking drugs, but Shaun stopped listening to me, like I say, when we were still kids. I found out what he was up to through our father, whose only contact was through mutual friends over there. I take it the straight and narrow path didn't last long?'

'No.' Having waded through the factual aspect of her relationship with Shaun, she now screeched to a halt. The personal stuff was still too raw for her to expose in a storybook fashion, as though nothing she was describing had actually happened to *her* or damaged her the way it had.

'So what happened?'

For the first time since she had embarked on her explanation, Vicky stood up and watched him from behind her chair with a shuttered, stubborn expression.

'I'd rather not wade through all of that,' she muttered.

'Why not?'

'Because it's irrelevant.'

'I happen to find it highly relevant.'

'Why? Aside from assuaging your curiosity, why do you care about the nuts and bolts of what happened between me and your brother?'

Max could feel his anger, previously abated, spring back into life with a vengeance and he gritted his teeth together. 'You were the last to know my brother, to see him, and, whatever happened in our pasts to sour our relationship, I'd still like to try and find out what was in his mind when he died.'

'Well, I can't oblige,' she muttered, flushing. 'What matters now is how we deal with this…situation…'

Max's voice was cold when he spoke. 'You're out of a job. That's the first step to *dealing with this situation*. You do realise that, don't you?' He didn't give her time to answer his rhetorical question. 'And I won't be supporting my niece financially from a convenient distance. Close up and personal. That's the role I intend to play.' His mouth was a grim line.

'I never said—'

'You don't need to. Whatever you claim your motives were, whether or not you intended me to find out about her, I suspect that the thought of money winging its way through your front door would compensate for the loss of your job.' He stood up and walked slowly around the room, pausing to glance at the occasional ornament or book lying on the shelf, while she watched him in appalled fascination. He had stripped her of her job, which was absolutely fine as far as she was concerned, but she could feel him gnawing away at her dignity, moving in leisurely, threatening circles, giving her only enough breathing space to be terrified of what might come next.

'I can survive happily without your money,' Vicky bit out sharply. 'And, just for the record, your brother gave me nothing towards his daughter. I've managed on my own for years and I can carry on managing.' She could feel tears pricking against her eyelids and she blinked them rapidly away.

'All the right sentiments.' He turned to face her. 'They might sound good coming from someone else.' He trailed his finger along a shelf, in the manner of someone checking for dust. 'So here's our little problem. Out of the blue, I have a niece, someone who deserves to carry the family name. I don't intend to run away from my responsibilities, such as they are, which means an investment of time as well as money, and, please—' he held up one hand to cut off the heated protest forming on her lips '—spare me the aggrieved pride. As far as I can see it, everything has a solution and here's mine. My niece inherits the family name and so, on an incidental basis, do you. I'm proposing to marry you.'

In the stunned silence that ensued, Vicky's expression went from shock to incredulity and finally to hilarity. She burst out laughing. She laughed so much that she found herself gasping for breath. Her eyes were streaming and in the absence of a handkerchief, she dabbed them ineffectively with the bottom of her shirt..

'I fail to see the joke,' he said tightly, which set her off again and when the hoots of laughter had finally subsided into little hiccups, she sobered up enough to say,

'Of course I won't marry you.' There had been nothing funny about his proposal. Her reaction had been one of delayed shock at finding her foundations rocked, but the thought of marrying him, when she of all people knew that heartache of relationships that exist without love, filled her with a deep, unaccountable sadness. She also knew that any liking, affection, the most remote of warm feelings towards another human being, could tarnish rapidly under the glare of a forced situation, a relationship created for the wrong reasons and endured for the sake of something or, in this case, someone. 'We don't love one another,' she said, and another stab shot through her, but this time the bitter stab of unrequited love. 'So what would be the point?'

'The point would be legitimising my niece; the point would be to create a stable environment for her.'

'The point would be that we'd be miserable, and misery doesn't make for stability.'

'How do you know that? If I recall, we were compatible enough...on more than one count.'

'That was then, before all of this...blew up.' She didn't want to be reminded of precisely how compatible they had been, and it went beyond sex and physical attraction. Despite her wariness, and despite all the voices in her head that had daily lectured to her on the unsuitability of the man, she'd found herself drawn to his personality, seduced by his mind. She'd surrendered all her defences for the transient pleasure of enjoying his humour and his intelligence, which made his ferocious hostility now all the more painful. 'You lead a fast bachelor life. You can't just take a wife and a child on board at the snap of your fingers! Don't you understand what a handicap that would be for you?' She watched the hard set of his features and felt a simmering anger. 'Your own brother couldn't even countenance the thought of having his life churned up by the arrival of his own flesh and blood.' She hadn't wanted to drag a rational conversation back into the personal battlefield that was her past with Shaun, but somehow she couldn't help herself. 'Oh, he *saw* his daughter, when it suited him, but she was never allowed to call him *Dad*. He didn't like what that word did for his fast-living image.' She laughed shortly.

'I'm not my brother,' Max told her with deliberate, cool emphasis, 'despite the similarities.'

'I won't marry you. If you want to see Chloe now and again, then feel free, but that's it.' Another spark of inspiration came to her. 'Aside from all the reasons I've given, do you realise that you might not even get along with her? How many children have you played with recently?'

'I don't see what that has to do with anything,' he muttered, flushing darkly.

'I guess that means *none*. You might *hate* children.'

'I think I'd know whether I did or not.'

'How? If you've never had any contact with them?' Now it was her turn to fire staccato questions at him. 'They can be clingy. They can whine and nag and they're no good around expensive clothes and furnishings. They constantly need juice, and mealtimes can be a battlefield. And I haven't even started yet...'

'I'm sure—'

'That you could manage? That's a *very* sweeping assumption!'

'So would you suggest that I get to know Chloe?'

'That might help.'

'What does she like?'

'What do *most* kids like? Junk food. Mickey Mouse. Outdoor fun.' She almost smirked at the thought of Max Forbes, impeccably dressed and leader of men, having outdoor fun with Mickey Mouse while consuming some chicken nuggets from a box. Did he even know who Mickey Mouse *was*?

'So let's take her to Disneyland. I'll get the hotel and flights booked and let you know the where and when.' He strolled towards the door while she remained open-mouthed and gaping at this neat turnaround of events. He shrugged at her expression and opened the sitting room door. 'Don't look so stunned. You put the idea into my head. You could almost say it was *your* idea. And don't get up. I'll see myself out.'

CHAPTER NINE

HE WAS determined. That much Vicky could acknowledge. He had given her four days in which to sort out her life, and now ten days in Disneyland: a holiday guaranteed to win the hearts of most children under the age of ninety. Even before they'd boarded the plane at Gatwick airport, she'd felt powerless in the face of her daughter's excitement.

Chloe had digested the fact that the man bearing a striking resemblance to her father, the man providing this sudden and hugely expensive treat, was her uncle. But, even so, on the trip over, as they'd sat next to one another, Chloe mistakenly lapsed into calling Max 'Shaun' a couple of times. Vicky, sitting in the aisle seat across from her, had winced as she coolly but firmly corrected the error.

Over her daughter's head, Max had caught her eye and said innocently, 'Never mind about that. She's only a baby. Can't help making the odd mistake and, face it, Shaun and I *were* twins.'

'Yes, but...' Vicky persisted.

'He's nicer than Shaun,' Chloe pointed out thoughtfully, 'don't you think, Mum? Shaun could be *scary*.'

'I think you've smudged just *there* on your colouring,' Vicky said by way of distracting her daughter, but she was aware of Max, still staring at her, ears no doubted pricked up and alert to continue Chloe's conversation.

'Haven't,' Chloe said, concentrating on a non-existent smudge.

'Well, you might,' Vicky said inconsequentially, 'so you'd better make sure you give it all your attention.'

That had been the day before. One whole flight followed by a meal at the hotel, during which she'd barely managed to get a word in edgewise.

Yes, Max Forbes was definitely a determined man. He was obviously determined to make an impact on his niece and he'd succeeded in a matter of a few hours—proving, Vicky thought with grudging admiration, how fickle children were. He'd won Chloe over with an unforeseen ability to enthuse over all things Disney, to express an interest in Barbie and the advantages of having a Barbie Ferrari bought for her for her next birthday, and topped it off with an uncanny knack of making sure that his colouring on the plane had been inferior to hers. Over a hamburger and fries meal, he had winningly offered to relieve her of her tomatoes and lettuce, and, by the end of the short evening, he'd left one child eager to see him in the morning and one mother who felt as if the ground under her feet had turned to quicksand.

'We'll have to get going early in the morning,' he'd murmured to her as they'd left the restaurant.

An exhausted Chloe was draped over Vicky's shoulder, so her pace of walking was painstakingly slow. No swift escape from the disturbing presence at her side. Unfortunately. Because the more she saw of him with her daughter, the deeper in love she fell. She had watched covertly, looking for signs of the mask slipping, but there had been none. He seemed delighted with Chloe, and she wondered, briefly, whether his joy with her as well as his feelings of responsibility towards her were tied up with his own feelings for the brother now lost to him for ever. She wondered if he was trying, through Chloe, to make amends for family differences that would never now be put to rest.

More to the point, Vicky wondered—and agonised—that if Chloe continued to be enraptured with him, she would find herself well and truly trapped in a situation she'd never foreseen.

'How early?'

'Before eight. If we're to get on the good rides. Which park do you want to go to first?'

'Park?'

'Didn't you read the guidebook I gave you?'

'Not much,' Vicky admitted, breathing a sigh of relief as the elevator doors opened. They were staying in the same hotel, but fortunately on different floors, an inconvenience for which the hotel had apologised and for which she was deeply grateful. The doors closed on them.

'You seemed to be absorbed in it when you weren't playing with Chloe.'

Absorbed on the one page, she thought, refusing to meet his eyes. Too busy concentrating on the man standing next to her to get any reading done.

'Here, give her to me. I'll take her the rest of the way.' He removed the barely stirring child to him before Vicky could protest. 'I'll meet you at seven-thirty for breakfast.' He stroked the dark head on his shoulder, then stood back to allow Vicky to pass as the doors slid open onto the luxuriously carpeted corridor.

The hotel was mightily expensive, with two sprawling halves which both shared a fabulously child-friendly pool, complete with fake sand.

'I suppose so.'

'And then we can go to the Magic Kingdom first. Get there before the crowds start amassing.'

They arrived at the bedroom door and Vicky stuck in her credit card-style key and pushed open the door before turning to him.

'You can hand her over now.'

He swept past her, through to one of the double beds which had been turned back and laid Chloe on it; then he proceeded to look critically around the room. 'Not as big as I'd expected,' he told her, folding his arms.

'More than big enough for the both of us.' Vicky stayed firmly positioned by the door, in the manner of someone willing an uninvited guest to depart.

Max moved slowly towards her, then, when he was about to leave, said casually, 'What did Chloe mean when she said that I was *nicer than Shaun*? Did he hit her?'

'No,' Vicky answered, startled by this abrupt shift in the conversation.

'What about *you*? Did he ever hit *you*?'

She hesitated just fractionally too long before responding with an unconvincing, 'No.'

'Why did you put up with it?'

Vicky looked over her shoulder, but Chloe was sleeping with unladylike abandon on the double bed.

She'd kept the lights turned off so that her daughter would not wake up, but she now wished that she hadn't, because the darkness imbued their conversation with a level of confidential intimacy that frightened her.

'When did it start? Were you pregnant at the time?'

'He wasn't a serial beater,' she said in a low voice. 'In fact, he only really lashed out at me twice. The first time was when I told him that I was pregnant and the second time was when I told him to stay away from me, after Chloe had been born. But aside from that he was—'

'The perfect partner?'

'Does it make any difference now?'

'It wouldn't if the past didn't play such an influential part in our lives. You can't imagine that by refusing to discuss it it all goes away, like a bad dream.'

'I'm not implying that that's how I feel...'

'Then talk to me, Vicky.'

'Why? Because you're on a mission to bond with my daughter and you think that you might as well bond with me as part of the deal?'

'Because,' he said levelly, 'I want to know.'

Because, she thought bitterly, *you anticipate a long time of seeing me ahead of you if you're to maintain contact with your niece, in which case you might as well smooth the way between the two of us.*

'Why didn't you tell him to leave you alone?'

'Because he threatened me,' she said flatly. 'Because he said that his daughter belonged to him and, if I didn't play along, he would make sure that his powerful family knew of her identity and they would move in to take her away from me. Fool that I was, I believed him.'

She heard Max's indrawn breath and steeled herself not to respond.

'It was always Shaun's way to prey off people weaker than he was. He liked to be in a situation he could control,' he murmured, more to himself than to her. 'You were young and vulnerable and he took advantage of the fact.'

'But I'm not young and vulnerable any longer,' she reminded him stiffly.

'Which is just as well. The young and vulnerable hold no charm for me whatsoever.'

With which he'd left her, awake and wondering what he'd meant by that remark. Had he been trying to tell her that *she* held a certain amount of charm for him? Or had it been a general statement which he had made without thinking? Or maybe he'd just been trying to point out yet one more difference between him and his brother. The permutations were endless, and by the time she'd finally fallen asleep she'd been nursing a mild headache from the sheer workings of her tired brain.

They both arrived at the hotel breakfast bar the following morning to find Max waiting for them, casually attired in a pair of deep green Bermuda pants and an open-necked, short-sleeved shirt in a dull cream and green check. Outside the heat would be building already. The weatherman—if the local weatherman was to be believed—had predicted a high of early eighties and had confidently assured her that the sky would remain blue and cloudless.

'Busy day ahead,' he addressed Chloe. 'Busy, busy day ahead. Lots of characters to meet, lots of exciting rides to go on. Have you even been to a fun park before? With rides and roller coasters?'

'No,' Chloe said. 'But I *have* seen a clown.'

Max nodded gravely. 'Yes, that would be impressive as well, I'm sure.'

'And I *have*,' Chloe said, gaining momentum, 'been in that pretend racing car outside the supermarket Mum takes me to at home.'

'Oh, *that* racing car. Goes fast, does it?'

'Well, it's just *pretend*,' Chloe told him gently. 'It doesn't really go *anywhere*. Does it, Mum?'

'No, honey.' Vicky looked thoughtful and said in an equally gentle voice, 'But perhaps Uncle Max thinks that these pretend cars actually shoot off and go places.'

'Thank you for explaining that to me, *Mummy*,' he said, raising one eyebrow with amusement. 'I'll bear that in mind for future reference.'

She heard the laughter in his voice and maintained a composed face.

'So which rides do you want to go on?' he asked Chloe, taking a bite of croissant so that his mouth was instantly covered in buttered crumbs. The sight mesmerised Vicky, who imagined how enjoyable it would be to lick each crumb off. Individually. It would take hours. Or at least seconds, because her tongue would not be able to resist searching his out. That would be the hardest part of seeing him. The seeing and the wanting but the not being able to touch. The agony as she was forced to play the happy, jolly, pally game when her body hungered to be touched by him in a way that was very far removed from pally.

'All of them!' Chloe's face was slowly but surely becoming submerged in maple syrup, despite Vicky's best efforts at keeping it at bay.

'Even the Tower of Terror?' He made his voice go spooky and took another bite of his croissant, this time absent-mindedly licking one finger clean before wiping his mouth with his linen napkin. He had no idea how eerily alike he was to his niece. It was uncanny the way nature could take a shade of hair and a colour of eye and replicate both so precisely in another human being. Even the spacing between the eyes and the shape of the mouth was all Forbes.

'What's that?'

'You mean your mother didn't read the description out to you?'

'No, she didn't.' Two pairs of grey eyes bearing the same expression stared at her, and she couldn't help a smile.

'She's too young for that particular ride, Max. *You* can go on it on your own.'

'I shall have to,' he said indolently, returning his gaze to his niece's besotted face. 'However terrifying a ride is, nothing terrifies the great Max Forbes!'

'Nothing?' Chloe asked, delighted, and Vicky heaved a loud, conspicuous sigh.

'Well. Spiders. Obviously.'

'*I'm* not scared of spiders. Am I, Mum?' Chloe glanced across at her mother, allowing her face to be dabbed with a napkin in the process. This, Vicky thought, was the relationship she should have had with Shaun. They should have delighted in each other's company. Instead, his rare visits to see his daughter had been an ordeal of moodiness, shouting and, after fifteen minutes of fatherly affection, a rapid downhill run to indifference and finally irritation. He'd brought her gifts inappropriate to her age, then had become sulky when she failed to be delighted with them, while Vicky had hovered miserably in the background, not quite knowing what to do and wishing he would just leave. There had never been one pore in his entire body that had possessed anything of the ease with which Max was now enchanting his niece.

'Not the ones in books, at any rate,' Vicky said, smiling.

'I'm not scared of anything,' Chloe assured him, abandoning the remnants of her breakfast in favour of conversation, 'I'm like you! Can I go on the Tower of Terror? Please? Say yes! Say yes!'

'Absolutely not,' Vicky responded immediately. 'It's a...' She plucked the guidebook from her bag, opened it at the relevant page, and read, verbatim, '"...*terrifying plummet, guaranteed to scare the most hardened.*" Anyway, there's a height limit and you don't measure up, short stuff. Apart from which, that particular ride isn't at the Magic Kingdom, so you'll have to settle for something a lot less adventurous.'

Later, as they entered the fantasy world of the Magic Kingdom, Max said to her, 'And what about you? Ever been to a place like this?'

'Not quite.' She paused and looked around her. Ahead was the fairytale Disney palace, pale spires rising up to the sky. It was early, but already beginning to get crowded. 'In fact, I never went abroad until I was an adult. Not all of us benefitted from a privileged background, financially.' But her voice was lacking in acrimony. 'I *did* go to Alton Towers, though, when I was fifteen, and from what I remember it wasn't *quite* like this.'

Chloe, desperate to get going, tugged her hand. She was in a state of high excitement. Vicky thought that her daughter might just spontaneously combust from it if she didn't go on a ride quickly. Were there medical services on site for desperate ride-deprived children? She put the question to Max and they both laughed companionably. She could already feel her resolution to remain as distant and as objective as possible beginning to crumble.

This was what it was all about. Being dragged along by a child, with the sun shining and your heart bursting with love for the man by your side. Had it not been for several clouds on that particular horizon, she would have said that happiness was very nearly within her grasp.

Even thoughts of Shaun, when she *did* think about him, had lost their power over her. He'd melted away into a vague shadow, eclipsed by the dynamic presence of his very much alive brother. Had that always been the way? she wondered. She could almost feel a pang of sympathy for him now, an emotion that would have been unthinkable three or four months previously. His ghost had let her go, or maybe it was the other way around.

The morning was spent on rides, little, delightful rides, for which the queues were not as lengthy as the guidebook had led her to believe. The three of them sat in the little cars, with Chloe between them, and anyone seeing them would have thought that they were the archetypal nuclear family, needing only the dog and the family saloon car to complete them. They would have done a double-take, had they heard the convoluted history behind them.

And was it her imagination, or had all that hungry, masculine lust bitten the dust? Ever since he'd found out about Chloe, the sexual interest he'd had in her had died. He was behaving with such wonderful ease, was chatting to her in such a friendly and unthreatening fashion, that she wanted to burst into tears. Instead, she forced wide, bright smiles onto her face until the muscles in her jaw began to ache from the strain of it. Over lunch, she watched him from under her lashes, watched the way his attention was focused on his niece, winning her over. When he looked at *her*, he wasn't seeing her as a woman, he was seeing her as Chloe's mother. With all the cards on the table, she couldn't have hoped for a better situation, nor could she have expected to be feeling as desolate as she was now.

'You're getting red,' he said, as they headed towards the MGM studios.

'Thank you,' Vicky snapped shortly. An unsightly blush added more unwanted colour to her cheeks and further worsened her temper.

'And you've gone into a sulk.'

'I have *not* gone into a *sulk*.'

'What are you thinking?'

'I'm thinking that Chloe's having a wonderful time,' she lied, looking at her daughter, who was ahead of them by a few paces. 'I've never been able to afford many treats for her.'

'That needn't be a problem from now on.'

'Because she's got an uncle with a bottomless wallet to oblige her? In case you're interested, money causes as many problems as it solves, and I don't believe in flinging it at children willy-nilly.'

'Stop spoiling for an argument.' He looked sideways at

the angry tilt of her head, the tight mouth, and felt an irrational desire to smooth it all away with his fingers. He wanted to stroke her face and produce a smile, like a magician pulling a rabbit out of a hat. His feelings for his niece, unexpected as they were, had been remarkably easy to find, but for a man who'd never had a problem with women her damned mother was proving to be a brick wall. He'd made a decision to back away from her, to win her over without suffocating her with an arrogant need to get what he wanted, and he was baffled that she was so tangibly failing to respond. Even when he'd managed to bring a smile to her face her eyes had slithered away from his and found sanctuary in her daughter.

'I am not *spoiling for an argument*. Why would I want to argue with you?' She glanced at him and tossed her head, like a beautiful wild filly rearing up angrily against restraint.

Had it not been for Chloe skipping ahead, looking back every so often to make sure that she was still within the fold, he would have been seriously tempted to drag Vicky back to the hotel room and restrain her in any way he could. Which would have had her bolting off in the opposite direction. He couldn't win, could he?

'You tell me,' he said through gritted teeth. 'Do you resent me because your daughter and I get along? Are you jealous?'

'That's ridiculous!'

'Is it?' He didn't want to. At least, he knew he shouldn't, but he pulled off the band securing the end of her plait and wove his hand into her hair, relishing the soft fall around his fingers and tightening his grip when he felt her automatically try and pull away from him.

'What are you doing?' she breathed.

He dodged the question. There was no acceptably polite

way of telling her that he was fighting the urge to do something very physical and very satisfying with her.

'I am trying to get your attention.'

'Well, you're not setting about it the right way.' She gave her head a gentle tug, but abandoned the effort when Chloe turned around. Instead she forced herself to smile, and when her daughter pranced to them and held her mother's hand she was reduced to having his hand in her hair, caressing her head. What was he playing at? She heard herself chatting to Chloe, valiantly keeping up the pretence that her body wasn't on fire, as his fingers softened and finally his hand dropped to curl around her waist.

He could feel her body tense. He could also smell the expectancy there and it thrilled and frustrated him at the same time. It was as though he knew the numbers to the combination lock, but not the right sequence and, however much he jostled with the digits, he never quite managed to get it right. The gentle brush of her slight body against his thigh was a sweet, agonising reminder of how capable she was of tormenting him, without even realising it.

She had a quality of stubbornness about her and, even though he could work out its origin, he still found it exasperating. It was as if her gentleness had hardened through experience into bull-headed pride, which had a nerve-racking tendency to shift into place just when he thought that he was getting through to her. He glanced down and hungrily eyed the gentle bounce of her small breasts, two mounds pushing against her light salmon T-shirt. Under normal circumstances, their one act of lovemaking, which had been the most satisfying he'd ever experienced, would have naturally led to more, but she'd dug her heels in and was continuing to dig her heels in.

By the time they had made it to the MGM studios, his

imagination had taken his frustration to new, unrewarding heights.

After some exhaustive queues for rides which Chloe seemed desperate to experience, they found themselves standing in front of the Tower of Terror, a massive brown house designed to look terrifyingly spooky. It succeeded.

'Bigger than I thought,' Max murmured dubiously. 'And no good for you, little one.' He patted the top of Chloe's head and she shot him a woebegone smile of acceptance.

'But feel free to go ahead yourself,' Vicky said, positioning herself opposite him just in case his errant hand decided to stray again. With Chloe there, she was compelled not to make a scene, which was the last thing she wanted to do anyway, when the feel of his skin against hers was sinfully exciting.

'I wouldn't dream of abandoning you two ladies…'

'Go ahead. We'll wait here for you.'

'The queue's too long.'

'Oh, that's all right. Never mind us. We'll grab an ice-cream and watch the world go by, won't we, Chlo?' She gave him a nasty grin and arched her eyebrows in feigned surprise, as though struck by a sudden thought. 'You're not *scared*, are you? Not when you told us that you were only scared of *spiders*?'

Max looked down at her and uncomfortably tugged at the collar of his polo shirt, as though it had unexpectedly shrunk two sizes and was now a tight fit. 'Why don't *you* have a go, if you're so daring?'

'Ah, so you *are* scared.' Vicky folded her arms and shot him a triumphant, lofty smile. This little nick of vulnerability was unbearably endearing, little did he realise. She noticed that he was looking positively sheepish and resisted the impulse to burst out laughing. 'I think I might just take you up on your offer, if you don't mind waiting for me...' Chloe's eyes went round with admiration.

'You wait,' he murmured into her ear, before she headed off to join the curling line of people waiting for the ride of their lives. 'When you stumble back here, white-faced and shaking...'

'Coward,' she murmured back with laughter in her voice, and she looked to find him grinning wickedly at her. Whatever ride she went on, she decided that it couldn't destabilise her more than the man standing in front of her. What man in all creation could make all her senses feel as though she was hurtling through space and could wreak havoc with her nervous system in a matter of seconds?

Forty-five minutes later, she discovered that when it came to matters of the heart she was hopeless, but when it came to rides she was utterly lacking in fear, and for the next week she exhaustively tried them all while Max and Chloe experimented with interactive playgrounds for pre-school children and rides that a three-month-old baby would feel at home on. Much to her glee. The one simulator ride he ventured on rendered him ashen-faced and speechless, and he was obliged to recover over a bag of chocolate chip cookies shared with his niece. He was good-natured in defeat and willingly allowed her to scamper off on mile-high roller coasters and death-defying water slides, while he tamely crammed his large masculine frame into ride-along cars and teapots and carousel horses with Chloe.

She discovered that they had settled into a habit of sorts, and one which suited her perfectly. They explored parks by day, a tiring business which left no time for personal chit-chat, had a spot of lunch, then went their separate ways in the early afternoon. Vicky had no idea what he hived off to do at two-thirty in the afternoon, but she suspected that he worked, having noticed that, despite the fact that the holiday had been designed for bonding with his niece, he'd still travelled over with his laptop computer. In the evenings, they both ate with Chloe, and then Vicky retired at a reasonable hour to bath her daughter, settle her and have an early night herself. The days were long and sleeping was no problem.

It came as a shock when she awakened on the Tuesday morning to the realisation that the holiday was virtually at an end. One full day left and they would be leaving the following night. She would have to start packing her stuff in the evening.

She couldn't believe that all the warnings in her head about caution and wariness had been for nought. Aside from the occasional reminder to herself that he could hurt her, she'd allowed herself to succumb to the magic of the place, just as Chloe had, without a thought for common sense. Aside from that one fleeting instance when he had touched her, with the safeguard of Chloe to let him get away with it, he had been the model of good behaviour. If anything, it had not reassured her of his worthwhile intentions but added to the growing list of reasons why she had fallen in love with him in the first place. Hostility was always a safer defence against surrender, but she'd failed to consider that it takes two to wage a war and, in the absence of a willingly antagonistic partner, she'd found herself suspending her despair and giving in to the moment.

He made it easy for her to laugh. He didn't give her the time or opportunity to dwell on her own personal problems and she'd discovered that it was remarkably easy to put off dealing with the complications of her life, of which he was a major one, until a later date. Some mysterious *later date*, when she would be forced to wake up and confront issues and handle the grief that she was busily creating for herself simply by enjoying him without the boundaries she knew were essential.

But she still imagined that she could somehow put off reality for the next two days, until he said to her, as they prepared to go their separate ways for the afternoon, 'We need to talk.'

Vicky took in the implacable expression on his face, browner now that it had been less than a fortnight ago, and felt a slither of foreboding crawl up her spine. 'How can we?' She shrugged helplessly, reluctant to let reality intrude on the last day but one. 'Chloe—'

'—has been fixed up with a babysitter for this evening. She's coming at seven-thirty. I arranged it through the hotel and, before you start throwing up your hands in anxiety, their babysitting service is very professional. They're all trained in childcare; I asked lots of questions before booking one. So we can have a meal and a…chat. It's time to sort out what we're going to do about the situation.'

Why did that have such an ominous ring about it?

Vicky wanted to ask *Already?* but she knew the dangers of even thinking along those lines, never mind voicing them. She also knew that he was right. If what he had set out to do with this trip was prove himself as a sound figure in Chloe's life, and a reliable, easy-to-digest one in hers, then he'd succeeded—if anything, rather well. He'd left her with no arguments to voice.

Chloe was asleep by the time the fresh-faced babysitter arrived, complete with a bag of 'things to do', which would not be used, and Vicky was more or less ready to go. Mentally bracing herself, and feeling a little strange in her first dressy outfit of the holiday—a small pale-coloured flowered dress in silky material, falling softly to mid-thigh, and a pair of wedge-heeled cream sandals that lent a couple of inches to her height. For the first time she felt nervous at the prospect of seeing him without the convenient distractions of Chloe and rides and people around them.

He was waiting for her at the bar, and it was a shock to see him, as well, more formally dressed. He was still wearing short sleeves, but his trousers were dark, and his bronzed skin gave him the appearance of someone of Italian descent. As she walked towards the table his eyes travelled once over her, then fell to his drink. He sat back in the chair, waiting until she had sat down, then called the waiter over to order a drink for her. In the silence that followed, Vicky nervously tucked her hair behind her ears, willing herself to feel the ease she'd felt with him over the past few days, but failing to find it.

'So—' he swallowed a long mouthful of his whisky and soda, then reclined back in the chair and watched her through brooding eyes '—glad you came after all?'

'It's been fun,' Vicky said, feeling like a candidate at an interview. She nervously accepted a glass of wine from the waiter and sipped from it. 'Tiring. Chloe's been ready for bed every night by seven. In England, I have to persuade her to climb under the duvet before quarter to eight.' She smiled at the thought of her daughter being cajoled into the dreaded bed.

'She's…a wonderful child. All credit to you.' He tilted his glass to her in a mock salute. 'From the sounds of it, you accomplished the near-impossible against all odds.'

'It wasn't as difficult as you make it sound,' Vicky informed him, gulping back rather more of her wine than she had set out to do and nearly choking in the process. 'I'm no saint, just one of millions of women who find themselves in a situation where they have no choice.'

'But you had my brother to contend with as well. My

brother with his threats and verbal abuse. And no money to cushion the future.'

'I never thought that my future needed cushioning,' Vicky lied valiantly. 'And I know where this is going. A long summary of my unfortunate past, followed by a swift recap of all the reasons why you should get what you want.' She'd known for a while that she had to recapture some of that lost hostility if she were to avoid complete emotional demolition. Now, she clawed and scrambled her way towards it, pretending not to see the hardening of his features. 'Well, it won't work.' She swigged back the remainder of her wine and it flared through her head like a bolt of white heat, then she banged the glass onto the table, extracting a few curious glances from the people sitting closest to them. 'You can see Chloe, of course you can, but within limits. Perhaps every other weekend. I don't want her life disrupted!'

'Don't you mean that you don't want *your* life disrupted? Don't you think that she deserves to know as much about her father's family as possible? Why deny her the heritage that's hers?'

'She's only a child! She doesn't know a thing about her heritage and doesn't care less!'

'But she won't be a child in ten years' time, will she?' he said venomously, leaning into her, his body rigid with anger. 'I wish to God,' he bit out furiously, 'that you'd fill me in on what your problem is! I'm offering you safety, financial security, an arrangement that's virtually foolproof and the best possible solution for the three of us!' He slammed his fist on the table and the couple closest to them got up and moved, giving them some very suspicious backward glances, 'What more do you need to be convinced?'

'I don't want *an arrangement*! I want...thunder and lightning...and fireworks...and magic!'

'Like you had with my brother?' he jeered. '*Those* kinds of *fireworks*?'

Vicky's face drained of colour and she stood up on shaky legs. 'I think I've heard enough.' She gathered up her bag and tried to gather up her lost self-control as well.

'Sit back down!' He lowered his voice to a demanding growl as the area around them cleared hurriedly. 'Running away won't solve anything!'

'There's nothing to solve!' She was bending towards him, her long hair hanging over one shoulder, her breasts heaving with emotion.

'Marry me and your problems will be over!' It was an order, not a request, hurled at her by a man whose eyes were flaring like shards of silver glass, his whole body taut with the desire to bend her to his indomitable will.

And he expected her to capitulate?

'Marry you and my problems would be about to begin!' She straightened, still shaking like a leaf. 'I'm going to pack. And you can do your own thing tomorrow. Chloe and I will stay here by the pool.'

'Listen to me' he commanded urgently, standing up, his long strides easily keeping up with her as she strode out of the bar.

'Why should I?' she threw at him. 'Because you're rich? Important? A Forbes?'

'Because there's something I need to tell you…'

'What?'

'You're being bloody stubborn,' he muttered.

'And *that's* what you want to tell me?'

'What's so wrong with being taken care of?'

'For the sake of maintaining your heritage?'

'Just answer the question!'

'I don't need you!' she told him, and herself, fiercely. 'I don't want to be *taken care of*. I'm more than capable of taking care of myself and my daughter! We're not *charity cases*!'

'I never implied that you were!'

'Then what *is* it you're implying?'

'I'm willing to give you—'

'I'm not interested.'

'Fine.' For a few electric seconds they stared in the darkness at one another, then he turned on his heel and walked away. Vicky followed him with her eyes until he disappeared around the hotel wall, then she too made her way slowly back to her room, not quite understanding why and how everything had gone so badly wrong, but knowing, somewhere, that open warfare was for the best.

CHAPTER TEN

WHY was it for the best?

She noticed that she'd somehow arrived at the gift shop, which was a grand affair with an alluring display case for every Disney product known to man. Or so it seemed. Instead of beating a hasty retreat, she found herself dawdling in front of the sweatshirts, ambling over to the array of postcards, indulging her train of thought.

Why, she thought, was open warfare for the best? Who was she protecting? Chloe? Not a bit of it. Chloe had accepted Max Forbes with the open enthusiasm of a child. Vicky was, she admitted, protecting herself, but how long could she go through life making herself pay for what had happened in the past? Where was the use condemning herself to a lonely future because she measured every man against Shaun and instantly backed away?

Max Forbes was nothing like his brother, aside from his physical resemblance, and even then there was something more finely honed about his face. It was as though nature had taken exquisite time with Max and then had done a rush job with his twin brother.

She strolled over to the stationery counter and absentmindedly registered that Mickey and Minnie were everywhere. On mugs, cups, paper, pencils. Spooky.

So what if he didn't love her? Was that the end of the world? Wasn't it better to have him in her life as a friend, rather than enemy? Because he *was* going to be in her life, one way or another. He wasn't going to just disappear and leave her to get on with things the way she always had.

She'd seen the affection in his eyes when he looked at Chloe, the curiosity of the world-weary man chancing upon something new and magical, the innocence of childhood. When he looked at his niece and saw the striking resemblance to him, he must feel a strong pull on his heart strings. How could he not?

So she could never have her ideal. Well, she wouldn't be the first in the universe, would she? And Chloe would have two parents rather than just her; a family, a sense of belonging.

A plump girl with amazingly white teeth and a broad smile walked across and asked her whether she could help, at which Vicky jumped and hurriedly grabbed a Pluto picture frame from the shelf and a box of writing paper which sported an intricate array of Disney characters leaping around the edges. Chloe would love it, even though letters, at this point in time, were solely addressed to her mother. With Max in her life she would now have two recipients for her three-line letters with their careful handwriting.

She left the gift shop and, instead of heading up to the bedroom to rescue the babysitter from her duties, made her way to the informal coffee shop that overlooked the pool for a cappuccino. As seemed to be the case in Florida, a simple cup of coffee was accompanied by something edible, in this case a vast butter biscuit dusted with powdery sugar. The actual cup of coffee was huge, and she realised that she should have specified a small cup.

The coffee shop was half empty, with a handful of couples sitting at tables in front of large dishes of ice cream. Most were poring over guidebooks, planning the remainder of their holiday with military precision. The décor was bright and jaunty. Not conducive to solitary meditation. But Vicky's mind, having broken its reins, was now unstoppable. It poured over the past and then leapt into the future and poured over that. There were so many permutations of what could happen that she felt dizzy, but the glaringly obvious thing was that she wanted Max in her life—she wanted his rich humour, his unexpected kindness, his wit, even the glimpses of ruthless cynicism that could have the other secretaries in the office running for cover. She loved every angle, every facet, every small nook and cranny of this man, and the thought of fighting him for evermore would end up destroying her.

She took a few more sips from her mug, managing to reduce the volume by very little, nibbled some more biscuit, like a mouse tentatively working its way around the outside of a piece of cheese, and then she stood up and dusted herself down.

Max would either be in the bar or in his bedroom. Presumably.

He wasn't in the bar. The prospect of going to his bedroom was a little daunting, especially when she wasn't quite sure what she was going to say once she found him, but her moment of brief hesitation was replaced by resolve and five minutes later she was knocking on his door. Her whole body was keyed to his response. She could feel every nerve stretching inside her.

When he pulled open the door, she was shocked by his face. He looked as though he had spent a night on the tiles. His hair was sticking out at odd angles and there was nothing cool and assured about his features. They were drawn, but his glittering silver eyes were as hard and shuttered as she had expected.

'What do you want?' he asked, standing in front of her, and her heart sank. She was beginning to forget what she wanted, and she realised that she hadn't even worked out what the heck she was going to say.

'I thought we might have a talk,' she said in a brave

little voice, looking up at him and fighting not to wilt at his expression.

'About what? Haven't you said it all? I must have been a damn fool to ever think I could batter down your defences. You've shut yourself away in your bitter little castle, and you're not going to let anyone get in, are you? Least of all the brother of the man who you think ruined your life.'

'He *did* ruin my life!'

'But that's in the past, isn't it? Or can't you accept that? Maybe you've grown so accustomed to being a victim that you've started to enjoy it. Oh, what the hell... I don't even know why I'm bothering to have this pointless conversation with you. Go to bed.' He half turned, preparing to shut the door.

'No!' she cried. 'Don't!'

'Don't *what*?' His eyes raked mercilessly over her.

'Don't shut me out. Please! Please?'

'Give me one good reason why I shouldn't. Isn't that what you've done to me?'

That expression of vulnerability brought a wave of tenderness over her that made her legs tremble. She hadn't thought that she was shutting him out. She'd been protecting herself in the only way she knew how, protecting herself against the possibility of ever being hurt again.

'Won't you let me in?' she asked quietly, reaching out and placing her hand flat on his chest.

She felt his body tense but she kept her hand there, needing the warmth of his skin through his shirt; then he turned away and rasped, 'Shut the door behind you.'

He stalked across to the small couch in the corner of the room and, her heart beating wildly, Vicky closed the door and walked across to his bed, and perched on the edge, crossing her feet at the ankles and loosely entwining her fingers on her lap.

She could hear the steady background hum of the air-conditioning system, which somehow only managed to intensify the silence between them.

He wiped his hands across his eyes and then looked at her, waiting for her to speak. She'd entered his territory and now it was going to be up to her to speak her mind, never mind the degree of receptiveness in the audience.

'I didn't mean to shut you out,' she began hesitantly. 'I didn't think I had, anyway. I mean, I came over here at your suggestion and you can't say that I've tried to monopolise Chloe's attention. In fact, I've hardly seen her at all these past few days!' Her automatic position of self-defence cranked into gear, but when she looked at him she discovered that it wasn't working with him.

'We're not talking about Chloe.'

'No,' Vicky murmured inaudibly. She drew a deep breath. 'I suppose...I suppose you're right. I went through a bad time with Shaun and I've let it influence my life. When I saw you...you brought everything back. I...it was like being hit by a roller coaster at full speed...I felt like my past was catching up with me again...and I was scared. Terrified, in fact,' she amended truthfully, reliving what she'd felt when she'd first set eyes on that familiar, yet not familiar face. 'I thought you were going to be just like Shaun. It didn't take long for me to realise...' Her voice wittered away into silence as she sensed dangerous ground ahead. Her fingers plucked at her skirt.

'*What?* For you to realise *what*?' There was a watchfulness about him that hadn't been there a few minutes previously and that was almost as alarming as his bitterness.

'For me to realise...that you weren't anything like

Shaun. Your brother was cruel, sadistic and addicted to getting his own way.' She couldn't sit still any longer and she stood up and walked jerkily towards the window and looked out, not seeing anything.

'And what was *I*?' he asked with mild curiosity. She could feel him staring at her and her stomach responded by going into knots.

'Nothing like your brother,' was as far as she would go on that one, and for the moment he seemed to accept her staccato answer. 'I should have left as soon as I could. I had planned to, but...'

'But what?'

'But I...enjoyed the job. I'd spent months doing menial work to pay the bills and, even though I knew it was dangerous working for you in case you ever found out the truth about me, it was tempting to carry on doing it for a little bit longer, enjoying the challenge of a job where I had to actually think. Never mind the money, which was very useful. I was finally in a position where I could afford to spend a bit on Chloe and on the house. I was putting money aside. I told myself that soon I'd leave...and then...'

'Your past jumped up to bite you on the hand when you were least expecting it. Another shock to your system, no doubt.' His voice was laced with jeering cynicism and for a brief second her eyes flashed angrily at him. He was deliberately making this hard for her, but what could she do about that?

'Yes,' she answered meekly, and he shot her a darkly challenging look before glancing away.

'So tell me why you've come,' he said, mildly curious now, not giving an inch. 'To prove right the old adage that confession is good for the soul? Nothing further to add to the litany of past regrets?'

'To tell you that I've been a fool,' she said with a shuddering sigh, and this time there was something different when he looked at her, although his voice was casual when he spoke.

'Oh, yes? And why would that be?'

'Because...' Her voice faltered now that she had hit the thin ice patch and risked falling in. What would he do if she confessed that she was in love with him? Would he laugh? Look embarrassed? Launch into an immediate retraction of his offer of marriage with the threat of real emotion entering into the equation, messing up his tidy little convenient proposition? None of these possible scenarios did anything for her self-confidence.

'Because...what?'

'I've thought about what you offered...' she began again, veering away from one patch of thin ice towards another. 'You know...your proposal...'

'What makes you think that that still stands?' he asked indifferently, though his eyes were still narrowed and watchful on her.

'I'm sorry...I thought...'

'But let's just say, *hypothetically*, that I was still prepared to enter into an arrangement with you.'

'Well, talking hypothetically,' Vicky volunteered nervously, 'I've realised that I would be prepared to go through with such an arrangement. I've looked at the way you are with Chloe...unless it was all one big act...'

'I don't pretend things I don't feel,' he responded grimly, and she wanted to scream at him, *Well, what do you feel about me? Aside from the occasional burst of lust? Anything at all?*

'In that case, I think it might be a good idea. I know it's not an ideal situation...' She smiled wistfully, imagining what the ideal situation would be. 'But it could work…'

'And I've been thinking as well.' His voice was serious, and she knew what he was going to say even before the words were out. It was like having a bucket of freezing water poured over her. 'I can't marry you, Vicky.'

'No. Well. Fair enough.' A great well of despair washed over her. 'I…that's fine… It was stupid of me to have resurrected that old proposal anyway. When we get back to London we can work something out…I know Chloe would be heartbroken if she didn't see you again…' Her feet, which were desperate to get her to the door, seemed to have been nailed to the floorboards. Amazing. She almost groaned with the frustration of it.

'Don't you want to know *why* I've changed my mind?'

'No…really…it's enough that you have…' She heard the misery in her voice and cringed.

'I've been doing some thinking of my own,' he said quietly, leaning forward and resting his elbows on his knees. He swept his fingers through his hair, but continued to stare at the ground until she eventually sidled a bit closer to him—because, if she didn't, she wasn't sure she would be able to catch a word he was saying. Not that he'd begun to say anything at all.

She felt a little braver now that he wasn't staring at her and reducing her thought processes to pulp. 'There's no need to explain anything to me. I mean it.'

'There is.' He favoured her with a brief glance, then he resumed his peculiar inspection of the carpet, as though he was looking for something he had misplaced there. His vocabulary, from the looks of it, she thought, which appeared to have deserted him completely.

The seconds dragged into one minute, two minutes, five minutes, until she said edgily, 'Well, explain away, then.'

Her remark was greeted with another quick look, too quick for her to read the expression in his grey eyes.

'If you've been watching my interaction with your daughter, then I've been watching yours, looking at the way you two reach out automatically for one another, the way Chloe looks across to you every so often for support...and you were right. Marriage and family is about more than arrangements and practicalities. It's more than a business proposition, two people adding up the pros and cons for living under the same roof, sharing the same house and then trying to work out whether it'll be worth the effort.'

His words jabbed into her like the blades of a knife, and every jab was accompanied by a sharp twist.

'I've always been sceptical about love; I've seen too many friends start out with hope and end up with ashes, and your relationship with Shaun was just another example of why emotion never gets anyone anywhere. Or so I thought. The fact is, emotion is all we have, and without that marriage is a sham, a hell on earth. It takes more than a lack of argument to make a good marriage, just like virtue isn't necessarily a lack of obvious vice.' He sighed deeply and raised his eyes to hers. 'Hence my change of mind.'

Vicky's head felt as though it was stuffed with cotton wool. The inside of her mouth wasn't faring much better either.

'Are you trying to tell me that you don't love me?' she said in a high, flippant voice, to defuse the situation which was threatening to overwhelm her. *Remind me,* she thought, *never to ask someone for honesty. Much better to avoid it at all costs.*

Instead of finding answering relief in his eyes, he didn't say anything.

'I'm not saying anything of the sort.'

His words dropped into the silence like bombshells. First of all she thought that she'd perhaps heard incorrectly, then it occurred to her that she'd misinterpreted what he had said. Hadn't there been a double negative in there somewhere? Lastly, she figured that perhaps it was just an elaborate counter-bluff, maybe containing a pun, although his face was unsmiling. A wash of unaccustomed colour stained his cheeks, but he was still holding her gaze, waiting for her to say something.

'Then what *are* you saying?' she asked into the oppressive silence. More requests for honesty, she thought numbly, could only end in tears. Hers.

'I'm telling you that I love you and I can't put you through a marriage that's one-sided. I thought,' he carried on, now addressing his fingers, 'that I could show you how much…how much I…well, you know what I'm saying here…' His flush deepened and his voice was unsteady, as though every word was an effort. 'I…but it hasn't worked…and…'

'So you're saying that *you love me*?' She could feel the wild stirrings of hope pushing through her woolly-headed brain, and as fast as she tried to shove it back it resprouted. Her heart was thundering inside her.

'I'm saying that I love you, Victoria Lockhart.' This time his voice was steady and his eyes never left her face.

She smiled slowly and went to sit alongside him on the sofa. 'Would you mind very much telling me that over and over again, because I'm finding it difficult to take in?'

He carried on looking at her, and suddenly the humour was back in his eyes.

'Now, why would I do that?' he drawled, sitting back on the chair so that he could have an all-encompassing view of her. From the expression on his face, it was a view he liked.

'Because I seem to have spent my life searching for you and I need you to tell me that my love for you is returned. You forget, I'm a woman whose self-esteem has taken some battering in her life...' Her self-esteem had never felt better. When she thought of Shaun and the emotional mess she'd been, she had the unreal feeling that she was thinking of a different person altogether.

'Well, there might be a bit of a price to pay...'

'What kind of price?' She looked at him with wide-eyed innocence, but there was a wicked smile on her face that matched his.

He leaned forward, curled his hand around the nape of her neck and pulled her to him, then he proceeded to kiss her thoroughly, only stopping to say into her hungry mouth, 'The marrying kind of price...' His tongue dipped back into her mouth and she laughingly struggled her way out of the heady embrace.

'There's no need,' she said, pink-faced but serious. Her hands pressed against his chest and she could feel the movement of his heart beating against his ribs. He reached to clasp both hands in her hair, on either side of her face, while the soft pads of his thumbs stroked her temples, her eyes, her cheekbones. Her small breasts ached for the same soft, seductive caress. 'I know that your sense of duty and responsibility prompted you to propose originally, but...'

'If only you knew,' he murmured, now stroking the slender column of her neck, then travelling inexorably downwards to cup her jutting breasts.

'If only I knew...what?' Her words ended on a gasp as he unbuttoned her and scooped her breasts out of their lacy bondage, rubbing his thumbs erotically over the raised tips.

'When I proposed to you,' he said, stilling his fingers

so that he could capture every ounce of her attention, 'I meant it. I *wanted* to marry you. I was determined to claw my way to your love if I had to die in the process. And now, my darling...' His fingers resumed their expert manipulation of her breasts, sending a convulsive shudder through her body. 'I don't intend to let you go. Ever.' He dipped his head to trail the tip of his tongue delicately around her nipple, circling, touching, flicking, until her unsteady breathing became small moans of pleasure. 'I *want* to marry you, just like I *want* Chloe to be a daughter to me, like she's a daughter to you...' He suckled on her breast, just long enough to make her slide a few centimetres down the sofa, long enough for his hand to gently curve around her thigh, massaging the willing flesh and edging upwards.

'And then, who knows?' He looked up at her and his grey eyes were dark with passion and tenderness. 'More babies?' He nuzzled her and she could feel him smiling into her breasts. 'If you thought you'd found the archetypal tycoon, then, my darling, you were wrong, because the prospect of domesticity has never seemed so good...'

'Are you telling me that I've tamed a tiger?' She watched his dark head against her body and was thrillingly, sinfully happy.

'Not,' he said, shifting his body so that he could unzip his trousers, 'completely. In one very important aspect, my love, you'll never be able to tame me...'

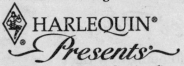

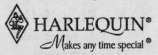

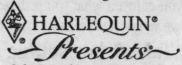